Make You A Woman

(By Vanessa Orr Francis)

Make You A Woman

http://vanfran.weebly.com

25602 Alicia Parkway #224

Laguna Hills, CA 92653

ISBN (978-0-692671399)

Illustration by Anderson Jackson

Printed in USA by CreateSpace

Follow the author on Facebook

Dedication

This book is dedicated to Gladys Lurleen Winton Curry and Bernice Ruth Orr Brown in appreciation of their "Herstories" that never got told. The pages are penned in gratitude for their courage and survival skills in a world aligned against them.

READER REVIEWS

"What a powerful read! I found myself identifying with a few of the characters. The writing.....creative, easy, and colorful. The storyline.....brilliant and captivating."

"The sample that I read reminded me of my favorite author. The structure of the chapters and the word choice was very consuming."

"The use of vivid descriptions and details are exceptional. The setting and situations are authentic to the historical nature of the area."

"I love, love, love it. I cannot wait to purchase the book and finish reading it. Thank you for such a wonderful book!"

Acknowledgements

To those who contributed along the way, I thank you and appreciate your kindness and encouragement. Sherri Williams for your gift of an online publishing class; Freda Freeman for your copyediting and proofreading skills which I could not have done without; Annette Winters for your reviews and essential critical comments; Tanya Hutchinson for valuable resources; Anderson Jackson for graphic art assistance; Lorena Farrell who provided the first review and who passed away before "Make You a Woman" saw the light of day, rest in peace; and REACH Community Church where I learned the real meaning and message of forgiveness.

To my daughter, Dionne Orr, thank you for being the inspiration that led, finally, to the finished work.

Everybody has a story. Make You A Woman is the fictitious story of five generations of women in one southern family.

It is a story about the secrets, shame and silence that destroyed lives and hindered the growth and development of talented women. It is a story of tragedy and triumph as the women overcome all obstacles to walk, finally, in the light of freedom and blessings!

Make You A Woman was written to encourage and uplift women who are going through or have gone through the indignity of molestation.

You are your own woman! Claim that truth and move to break every chain in your life that seeks to entrap you.

Vanessa Orr Francis

Table of Contents

Section One

Section Two

Section Three

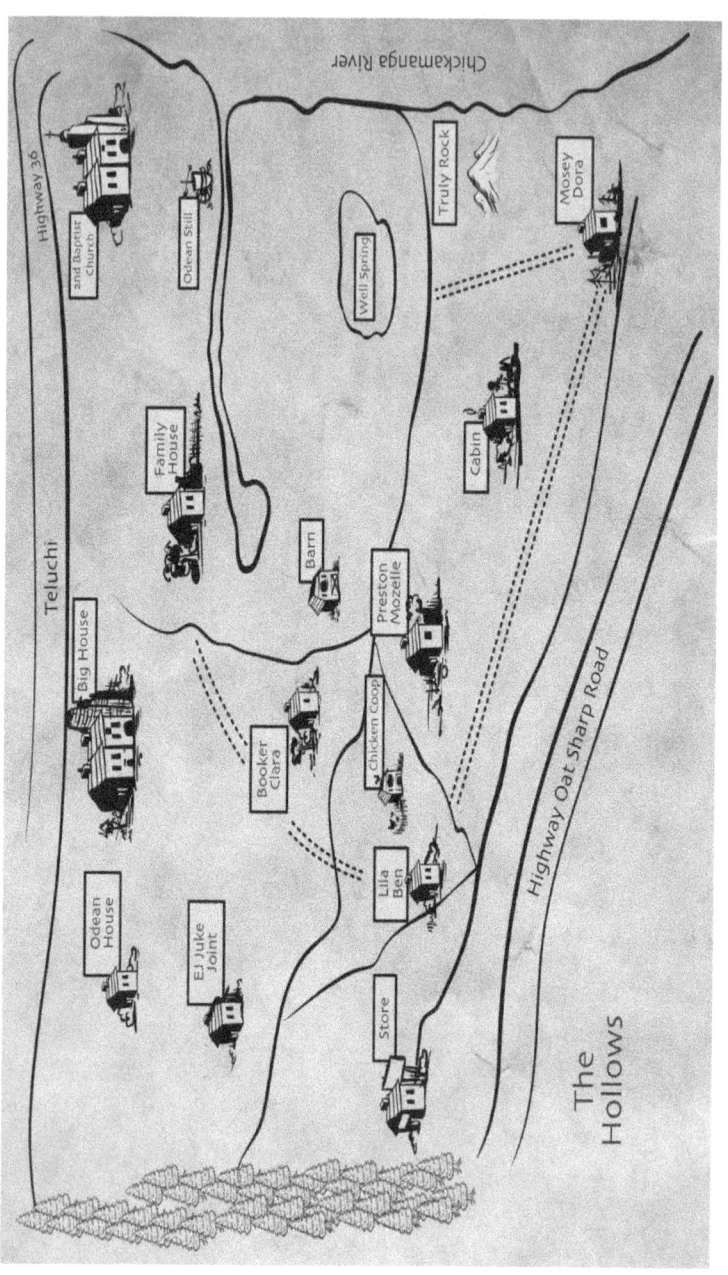

Chickamanga River

Highway 36

Teluchi

2nd Baptist Church

Odean Still

Well Spring

Truly Rock

Mosey Dora

Family House

Cabin

Barn

Big House

Preston Mozelle

Booker Clara

Chicken Coop

Lila Ben

Odean House

EJ Juke Joint

Store

Highway Oat Sharp Road

The Hollows

GHEE
FAMILY TREE

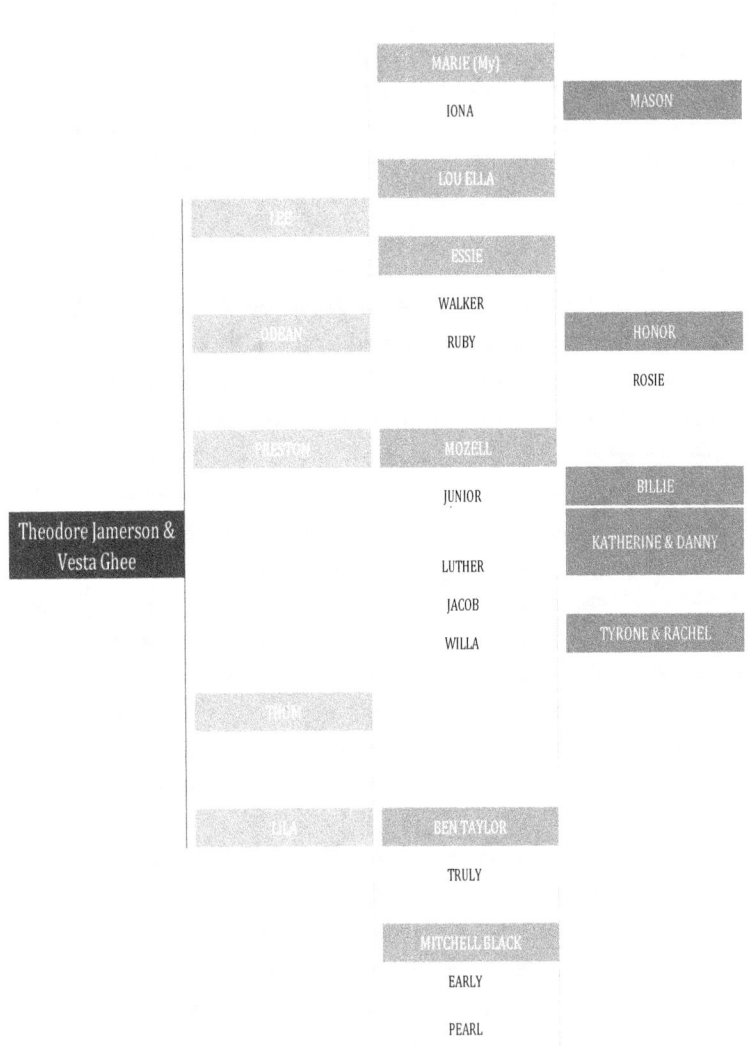

		MARIE (My)	MASON
	IONA		
		LOU ELLA	
LEE		ESSIE	
	WALKER		
ODEAN	RUBY		HONOR
			ROSIE
PRESTON	MOZELL		
	JUNIOR		BILLIE
Theodore Jamerson & Vesta Ghee			KATHERINE & DANNY
	LUTHER		
	JACOB		
	WILLA		TYRONE & RACHEL
THUR			
LILA	BEN TAYLOR		
	TRULY		
	MITCHELL BLACK		
	EARLY		
	PEARL		

Definitions

Hollow: Having nothing inside, not having real value or meaning, a place or area that is lower than the area around it, an empty space inside of something.

Honky-tonk: A local nightclub that specializes in drinking, dancing and local bands.

Juke joint: A small inexpensive establishment for eating, drinking or dancing to the music of a jukebox.

Home brew: An alcoholic beverage made at home; beer, wine, whiskey.

White lightning: Moonshine; a kind of alcohol illegally made, distilled corn whiskey.

Section One

INTRODUCTION

"Take the baby!" The midwife placed the tiny bundle, slippery with afterbirth, into my arms. The infant was awake but quiet; her eyes wide open, she glanced around but did not cry, whimper, or appear dazed by the birthing ordeal. She was as silent as the Alabama night.

"Yes, my pretty one," I cooed. "It's alright. Auntie is with you, all is well."

I carried the baby to a clean, cracked porcelain basin and washed her plump brown body with warm water. The water was soon so bloody that I could no longer see the faded roses at the bottom of the bowl.

After she was bathed, I laid her on a clean quilt spread out in a handmade oak cradle made just for this birth. The baby now appeared to sleep, a finger already between her lips. Still she hadn't cried out or made a sound; maybe she knew she'd soon be motherless.

Behind me I heard old Rhea, the midwife, mumble something to my mother. I wasn't alarmed because old Rhea mumbled all the time, except when she dipped snuff, and she never dipped snuff in the birthing room.

"Noooo! Please, God, no, no, no, no . . ."

I turned around as my mother raised her hands to heaven and to the God she said protected babies and fools. She screamed and collapsed onto one knee, arms still raised toward the ceiling of our wooden shack.

"Sorry, chile, she done bled so; you could wring out these sheets and get a pitcher full of her blood." Rhea knelt beside mama and held her. Mama kept on screaming to heaven, and to God.

All thoughts of the cute baby went out of my mind. I ran to the bed. My little sister Marie lay so still. I called her My, as in my heart and my love. Mama had to work most every day in the fields, from sunup till sundown. Ever since My was born, I plaited her hair, I nursed her through sickness and it was I who fed her when she was hungry. I was more mother to her than the one who bore us both.

"My, don't go. It's a girl!" The one I loved most in this hard and awful world had birthed a baby who would never know her. Marie was only 13 years old.

It wasn't fair for her to be lying in this bed with no future. She was so young, just a baby having a baby. The baby would be fine but my sister was in trouble.

"Don't you want to see your baby?" But I knew, as soon as I looked at her, that her time was up. Mama's God was calling. Marie's tiny brown face was sweaty and looked old and tired. When she shivered I pulled the old quilt up until it was underneath her chin, but she shivered still, and I stretched out on the bed and covered her frail body with mine.

On the floor beside the bed, Mama continued to howl and pray for a healing, or a miracle.

I held my sister's face between my hands, wanting to hold on to her for those last few seconds.

13

Her life flashed before my eyes. I saw the laughing brown bundle that toddled behind me as I hung clothes out to dry, stiff little braids that framed her face as she watched me feed the chickens and the ashy legs forever running, never walking. And lately the heavy, pregnant body that seemed so wrong for her childish frame.

"My. Please don't go, don't go, God, please don't." I moved her face from side to side, massaging her temples. As I cooed into her ear for the last time, I heard her whisper something to me.

"He said . . . he'd make me a woman . . . like you . . . 'Bye, Lou. . ."

I gasped in shock. With her final statement, I now knew who raped my sister, taking her innocence, taking her life.

I held on to her frail body, but she was gone.

*   *   *   *

A small group of men stood outside the juke joint; drinking white lighting from Mason jars. Hand-rolled cigarettes hung from moist, full lips. Smoke hovered above their heads like swamp fog. Someone inside the tin roof shack strummed an out-of-tune guitar; a bluesy tune whispered on the humid country night.

"Man, you crazy! Can't keep a thing on your mind 'sides women!"

Ham Johnson threw back his head and laughed at his own words. They all laughed, even Milas Green, the object of their scorn.

"But, I tell you, that high yeller gal sure do know how to make a man keep coming back for more!" Milas protested, and took another sip of white lighting.

"Yeah. How much of your field money you spending when you go back for more! And do she make you holler, more, more, more?"

"Do she say, ride me Daddy?"

The three men convulsed with laughter, slapping each other on the back, crying with glee of the imagined sexual conquest. They had come to the juke joint from the field, dirty, sweaty and now they were also drunk.

Somewhere up on the mountain a scream erupted, cutting through the men's laughter like a knife cutting across a hog's throat.

To a man, they backed up against the side of the juke joint. The cigarettes dropped from their gaping mouths. Mosey Thomas dropped a Mason jar of white lighting as he scrambled for the front door. When he reached out to open the door, it jerked opened from the other side.

"What in hell?" Emma Jane, known as EJ to her friends and customers, asked standing in the doorway of her juke joint as she confronted the frightened men.

The screaming went on and on, moaning sometimes, sometimes babbling. It sounded like someone or something,

15

the men couldn't tell which, was in an awful rage. It was a cry of desperation and pain; like the owner was insane or nearly so.

The three men outside and everyone inside the shabby, one-room building, held their breath, waiting for the screams to stop bouncing off the mountainside. Finally the cry became a moan and the moaning faded, as if the owner traveled away from them. At last it was quiet.

A full five minutes after the sounds stopped - Ham later said it had seemed like an hour - someone hiccupped and broke the spell.

"Sounded like screech owls crying, must gone be a bad winter."

"That weren't no screech owl, fool, sounded like the devil."

"Hope it ain't the Klan!"

"Naw, they don't make a noise till they burning your house down around you! Dirty cowards!"

"Sounded like a crazy man."

"Crazy woman!"

Milas, Ham and Mosey decided to go inside for another drink, or three, of moonshine. Standing outside had lost its appeal.

Everyone had something to say, and everyone felt uneasy. What had started out to be the usual drinking, gambling, funnin' night up at the juke joint had turned into a mystery. It could only be solved in some awful, painful way, probably for somebody colored.

They all hoped it wouldn't be someone they knew or loved. Up and down The Hollow folks heard the demented voice fade in and out throughout the night. Come morning, most people had heard parts of the story.

Poor Marie Johnson had birthed a monster baby and died. Old lady Rhea had poisoned Marie with one of her herb medicines and she had died. The baby was born with a caul over its head.

Whatever the rumor or gossip, the truth remained. Marie was dead. Her mama and the midwife laid the body out and called for Pastor Crutcher, who said he'd be there soon as he finished marrying up a couple over in Madison County.

Marie's sister, Lou Ella, had taken the baby girl and took off into the night; everyone said Lou had been howling all night long in grief over the loss of her sister.

The Johnson men and Lou's husband and his brothers organized a search of the mountain and the old Hollow Trail.

THE HOLLOW

The Tennessee Valley Authority made an offer to buy the remaining 25 acres known as The Hollow located in Morgan County, Alabama.

I was the designated heir; bequeathed the property in trust for the entire family by my aunt, Lila Black.

My ex-husband suggested I visit the area one last time before making up my mind about selling off the final link to my childhood. I already knew that I never wanted to again see the place that had been my legacy.

Now, after Aunt Lila's funeral, I stood on the land letting go of my past; it felt like alien territory.

The view of the creek and mountain where I'd grown up sent me reeling back into my unhappy, terrifying and often violent history.

The Hollow, as it had been known as long as I could remember, looked both beautiful and disturbing; like seeing the skull beneath the smiling picture of a beautiful woman. In this place I had always felt bad things could and would happen.

It was a beautiful day. The creek rippled by on my right-hand side. Pine trees, bamboo plants and elms lined the bank as far as you could see. Jutting out into the swirling waters Truly's Rock stood as it always had in defiance of the fact that it wasn't a rock; it was the largest boulder in the area, and it dominated everything around it.

As a child, before I learned how it got its name, I once tried to fish from the boulder's flat top. Everything seemed to go wrong, the mosquitoes were unusually active for that time of day, my fishing line got caught in the undergrowth and I lost my favorite bobber when I untangled the balky line. Finally, I caught a local scavenger fish known as a sucker, the most unappetizing fish that ever swam.

When I learned how the boulder got its name, I never fished in that area again.

The mountain loomed over the trail where I stood. Parts of it were so overgrown it was now impassable. It once connected the small rural Alabama communities of Vermosa and Teluhci.

Those small communities were not the only thing the trail connected. Old man Theodore Jamerson, to whom the original 120 acres belong, once ruled this land and divided it between his two families. In Vermosa, at one end of the trail known as The Hollow lived his black mistress and five children. His white wife and six children lived in their big plantation-style house at the beginning of the trail in Teluchi.

Jamerson added on to the original property in 1870. The new acres consisted of rolling hills of farmland, undeveloped woodland and peaceful valleys, all connected by numerous streams, ponds and a tributary of the Chickamauga River.

The Chickamauga River originated in Georgia and was the site of the defeat of Confederate forces under the command of General Braxton Bragg at the hand of Union

Troops led by Major General William Rosecrans. Local Indians named the river The River of Death.

In the early 1950s, Tennessee Valley Authority (TVA) purchased the remaining land not owned by Jamerson or Ghee heirs. Over the next 20 years, they also purchased most of that land as well. I was the only holdout. Selling my 25 acres would not only spell the end of one black family's near-century of land ownership, but also of The Hollow itself.

The TVA planned to dam the creek, level the rolling hills and turn the entire area into a protected game reserve. Perhaps it would be a fitting end. The mountain had already witnessed violence and bloodshed. In the end if it was used to protect life, that would be a wonderful way for the area to finally be at peace.

I tried not to come back to my birth land. Although my family and I paid the property taxes on time, I hadn't been to the area in more than 20 years. I came home every two to three years to visit remaining family and friends, but "home" was no longer located in The Hollow.

The fire had taken care of all that.

My family now lived, as country people say, in the big city. We moved to Huntsville after the fire. Only Aunt Lila, who recently died and left the land to me, still had a house in The Hollow.

Fire was supposed to cleanse and eventually renew.

That might be true, I thought as I looked around at my surroundings. I saw no traces of the conflagration that had sent me running for my life down the old trail with my clothes and hair on fire. The scars on my body eventually healed. Two small marks, one under my right arm, one under my chin, and a faint paleness of skin around my hairline were the only reminders of that night of horror. However, my heart and mind had been scarred forever.

Something moved behind me.

"Stupid, stupid woman, how could you forget where you are?" I hissed and started to back away from the looming trees, the overly bright flowers and kudzu vines choking the life out of everything else.

At my movement, a startled Blue Jay took flight. I sighed with relief and followed the colorful bird's flight across the clear sky.

The Blue Jay startled me into one of my earliest memories; a memory that belonged to a reality I had spent a lifetime trying to forget. Many things happened to me while I was growing up here, on this very trail and around that bend in the road. I glanced that way now, half expecting to see the man I killed when I was eight years old standing there hiding his hands in the pockets of bibbed overalls.

The past flooded my mind as I turned away from the mountain. I knew from experience that everything about my family and the past would continue to haunt me until I was drained and exhausted by the stories my ancestors had to tell.

It was time to get away from this place, forever.

THE BEGINNING

Theodore Jamerson won 40 acres surrounding his property from Rudolph "Rudy" Metcalf in a card game.

Rudy was the last of his line. Most of his friends felt sorry for the drunk, him being a Civil War hero and all. Someone claimed he'd even fought at the River of Death battle. Rudy never said; just kept drinking his life away.

Jamerson's friends wanted him to let "poor ole Rudy" pay him back. But Theodore just smiled and told them to mind their own business and he'd mind his. Rudy would lose everything sooner or later. Why not sooner, he thought, and why not to me?

The Jamersons already had 80 acres; the additional Metcalf land would give Theodore the rights to a creek, a mountain, and several choice field acres located near The Hollow. The area was prime, not only for its fertile fields but also because it was close to the colored community that worked the fields and sharecropped areas not deemed profitable for the landowner.

Jamerson wanted to be prepared to provide for a family. Once he had been at the bottom of the poor white trash heap and he remembered that feeling. No sir, he'd have none of that for his future family. He wanted above all to be a prosperous landowner and cotton baron. He had big plans for the land.

The family Jamerson imagined on that day when he won the Metcalf land in a poker game with three aces would prosper, and he would build a big plantation house on the valley side of his property in Teluhci. He and his wife, Lucille, would have six children in 10 years. The children would be healthy but he and Lucille would eventually drift apart.

Three of his children would leave home; Hazel and Janie married Yankees, and his oldest, Theodore Jr., went west to mine for gold and was never heard from again.

None of the three children who remained in the area would marry into families as successful as their siblings. Linda, the youngest, married a man who came from white trash. Buckley, "Buck", chose a woman from a local family, and they had three girls. Harley developed a strong taste for moonshine and women and would be killed by an irate husband come home too soon.

None of the Jamerson children took an interest in the farm or in their father. Lucille was not a farm wife and had raised her children to consider farming an unsuitable occupation. She wanted the boys to go to the University of Alabama and become professionals.

At the poker game that night Jamerson couldn't know how much his big plans would change over the next 35 years as he and Lucille drifted farther and farther apart and his children moved on with their lives.

He also had no idea that he would take up with the daughter of one of his father's former slaves and father five more children: four boys and one girl.

Eventually, Jamerson would become estranged from all of his white children and would live out his life with his half-breed mistress and children.

The Black Jamersons carried their mother's last name, Ghee, and they would eventually inherit Jamerson holdings. Preston, Odean, Lee, Thom and Lila owned property, houses and a country store. Envied by all other blacks in the area and hated by poor white trash, the secrets they harbored would ultimately destroy lives and haunt their children and descendants' for five generations.

VESTA'S STORY

When you got old and life was just about over, things finally didn't look so bad.

At least that's what Vesta told herself as she sat on her front porch, braiding her wiry long white hair. The hair was one of the things she inherited from her Creek father; that and the ability to face catastrophe with stoicism.

She'd seen it all. If God, the devil or your neighbor for that matter, decided to visit you with feast or famine, Vesta felt her family had always been served first at the famine table. Oh, they'd had some luck along the way; better off than most of the colored folk in the area, they were still land-poor. Her sons, who owned a small store that set at the beginning of The Hollow, fancied themselves storekeepers and merchants.

Vesta was proud of her whole family. The boys, Odean, Lee and Preston, ran a store, but she knew the wooden shack they called a store contained just a collection of odds and ends. They mostly sold handmade quilts, preserves and jellies that she and Clara, her daughter-in-law's mother, made. They also carried cane-bottom chairs and other simple furniture made by Hap Turner. Chicken feed, flour, molasses, crackers, bologna and other assorted basics rounded out the selection.

Credit for most of the store's business went to the white lighting and homebrew Vesta's oldest son, Odean, supplied.

Of course, those were the backdoor items sold mostly to men who worked hard, and drank hard; mostly field hands and other Negroes who needed credit. When a white man came in, he was usually lost and stopped in to ask directions. Locals bought goods at that new store in Teluhci.

The old lady sighed and fanned herself with her voluminous skirts.

It was August and hot, simple enough. Come August in the Deep South, it should be hot for old women, for babies and fools, too.

Vesta chuckled, remembering that her family also had its share of fools.

She remembered back when she and Theodore started stepping out together; her family became fearful of what would happen to her when she announced that she was pregnant with a white man's child.

She'd had dreams they could never understand. Dreams that one day land, money, and anything else she wanted would be hers for the taking. Vesta dreamed of being treated like a white woman, not like a half-breed not good enough to take out a piss pot!

She had not let anyone stand in her way. And when the time came, she did what she had to do to secure her children's future.

Everyone in her family worked for the Jamersons; such work as it was, sharecropping and yard work, mostly. None of them had more than two pennies to rub together.

The Jamersons themselves were just a step above poor white trash, but they did believe in working for a living. Theodore, the only child, had grown up wanting more out of life; at least in the beginning he'd had big dreams too.

After the Civil War, soon as things settled down, Theodore visited distant cousins down in Louisiana. He'd been gone just over a year and when he returned, he brought home a bride.

Vesta remembered that day with real pleasure!

The day "Miz Lucille" came to stay was the first time 10-year-old Vesta had ever seen so many dresses and real face powder instead of talcum. And jewelry! Miz Lucille had a box full of rings, earrings and necklaces of pearls and other stones that she wore all the time, not just on special occasions. Vesta stood in the doorway of Theodore's old bedroom and gawked like the country pickaninny she was.

Although at that time little Vesta had no thoughts of marrying Theodore or anybody else for that matter, she did sense that the young bride was not equipped for life as a country wife.

Lucille was a 17-year-old city girl, tall and pale, the kind of white that don't like sun, and she was not use to chores. In fact, Vesta thought to herself, "Miz Lucille can't do nothin' but sew useless little doilies!"

In private, Theodore's parents, as well as Vesta's folks, often expressed the same doubts. When the time was right, Vesta remembered all she heard about Miz Lucille and her inadequacies and found a way to turn it to her advantage.

27

The old lady, sweating in the humid southern day, finished braiding her hair and for a time concentrated on shelling the chickpeas in her lap for the evening meal.

*   *   *   *

"Smoke. Up you mule! Up I say!" Joe Ghee yelled at the animal and tried to restrain it from pacing between rows in the fertile earth.

"Damn animal's been actin' funny all day!" Joe stopped to rub his back and tried to keep Smoke under control at the same time.

Field work was never easy. No Lie.

"Yeah, Daddy, I saw Bessie lying down in the pasture this mornin'," Vesta said as she followed behind chopping up large clods of dirt that hadn't been plowed. "Last time I saw that we had frost in August."

"That sound bad, cows don't do that, 'less they sick. I think we should go in time we get to the end of this row," He shaded his eyes and looked up at the cast-iron sky. "Think it gonna rain. That's bad, 'cause we need to get this field plowed 'fore it come down like cats and dogs."

By the time they did get to the end of the row, the weather had changed for the worse. Clouds raced across the sky like children running from the whipping switch. Thunder, heard in the distance, seemed like it rumbled from the belly of heaven.

The rain streamed out of the clouds, coming down hard. Raindrops hit the parched ground like knives; kicking up puffs of dirt at first until small puddles formed.

"Vesta, let's get back to the barn 'fore we get drowned out here!" Joe said as he unhooked Smoke from the ancient plow and headed for the safety of the dry barn. "Look like a bad storm coming, bet it gonna storm all night."

"Go on, Daddy, I left Mama's quilt and the water jug under the pecan tree." Vesta turned to run toward the far end of the field they had only been able to half plow. "Don't worry 'bout me; if it rains too hard I'll take cover in the root cellar."

As Vesta raced across the field her family sharecropped for the Jamersons, she pulled her skirt up around her waist and tied the hem over one round hip.

Now 22, the once gawky girl had matured into a beauty. She had her father's high Indian cheekbones and long, straight nose. A reddish glow made her light brown skin shine like copper; she also had full sensuous lips, strong white teeth, and clear wide-set eyes that told the story of her mother's African background.

When Vesta turned 15 she caught the eye of every man in The Hollow, young, old, robust, crippled or sick. J.D. Bedford caught her eye. When she was 16 they married.

Two years later, she, J.D. and three-month-old Annie rode in the back of a wagon coming home from a shindig in Apple Grove when the horse was spooked. Both J.D. and the driver, Hills Brown, were drunk. J.D. was tossed out first, broke his neck and died instantly. The out-of-control horse plunged into the river. Hills, Vesta and Annie got thrown into the muddy waters. Vesta was hit on the head by a tree trunk and got tangled up in the branches; she barely survived, but lost her grip on Annie.

The young widow returned home to grieve and heal; an only child, her folks could use another hand in the fields. Now, three years later, she remained with them, childless and husbandless.

When Vesta reached the pecan tree she snatched up the tattered and wet quilt the family used to sit on as they ate lunch in the field. Today they'd had cornpone and salt-back. She grabbed the rag the lunch had been wrapped in, the water jug and turned toward home.

The low rumbling sounds from heaven turned ominous. A minute later lightning touched down in the field near the tree and skipped along the ground like a stone skimming the surface of a river. Vesta cried out and rushed for the safety of the root cellar, clutching the quilt and jug against her wet and trembling body.

Overhead the wind lashed out in fury. Lightning continued to slash at the field, the forest, and the running woman.

She fumbled with the latch on the old wooden door, her wet hands sliding off twice before she got it unlatched. Flinging the door open she rushed down the short steps and threw herself on the beaten-earth floor. She pulled the quilt over her head, hiding under the tattered pieces as she had hidden under the bedcovers at night when she was a child.

For a minute she couldn't move. Fear wrapped around her more than any quilt ever had. It had been a close call.

She heard wet slapping sounds above her. The wooden door was flung open then slammed shut against the violent storm. Footsteps crashed down the short steps, and before she could move something heavy dropped down on her and crushed all the air out of her lungs.

"What in hell!"

Vesta screamed as if the devil himself had stepped into the root cellar.

"Who is it?"

She screamed again until the heavy object lifted from her body. Soft rustling sounds filled the root cellar. A match was struck, illuminating the rows of canned vegetables, fruit preserves, and other foodstuffs the family prepared and used during the bitter winter months.

The match also revealed the shadowy face of Theodore Jamerson.

"Oh. Oh, Mr. Theodore, it's you." Vesta said as she hurriedly slid along the floor to a different area of the cellar. "I didn't know who it was."

"And I can see it's you Vesta, just quit your squalling 'fore you give me a god-awful headache," Theodore Jamerson frowned down at her huddled form for a minute before

31

turning and searching along the wood-plank shelves. The match went out.

"Shit fire, done damn burned my finger!"

Cursing and more rustling sounds filled the dark cellar. Finally another match was scratched into life and Theodore's search of the shelves turned up a kerosene lamp. He removed the sooty glass and held the match to the wick. A feeble light glowed, and got stronger.

Theodore shook the match out, placed the glass back on the lamp and held it up high to better view the other cellar visitor.

The kerosene light revealed a young woman in a clinging wet dress. Her full, round breasts strained against the top and were visible through the thin and damp fabric. The dress rode up her thighs revealing strong, well-shaped, muscular legs. The rainwater made them glisten in the lamplight.

Theodore groaned.

Vesta, thinking she must look like a wet cat, stood and gathered the quilt around her cold body.

"Don't," Theodore said in a husky strained voice and reached out for the quilt, "I mean . . . let it dry out first."

He took the quilt, shook it out and draped it over the shelves. He set the kerosene lamp down by the quilt and looked back at Vesta before holding his hand out to the warmth of the lamp.

"Come, Vesta," he said and held out his other hand to her. "It's warm over here."

*   *   *   *

The old woman shook herself, spilling some of the chickpeas. She realized she'd fallen asleep dreaming about the day she and Theodore first got together.

"Mercy, getting awfully lazy these days," Vesta yawned and stretched out in the cane-bottom rocker. "Gonna have to be put out to pasture 'fore long if I don't get some spirit."

The day was still hot; a slight breeze and lengthening shadows were the only indication that it was late afternoon.

Vesta noticed that she had not pinned up the long thick braids she'd recently finished plaiting. Still fussing at herself for being lazy, she took a few minutes to pin the braids up in full circles around her head.

She glanced through the open door to see if anyone was at home.

The house, as was most Negro homes in the South, was a shotgun affair. The hallway went from the front door to the back door with rooms along each side. This was the house Theodore had built, however, so it was larger than the homes of other coloreds in the area: six rooms, including three bedrooms, kitchen, parlor and dining room.

It was the first house or the last, depending on which access trail you used to get to The Hollow.

33

From where she sat, Vesta could see into the parlor, dining room and kitchen. A red-and-white checkered oilcloth covered the kitchen table, which held a sugar bowl, vinegar bottle with shaker top, hot sauce and salt shaker. If anyone had come home without waking her, they'd usually be back at the kitchen table.

"Well, still got time to cook these peas and some cornbread," Vesta said aloud, settling herself more comfortably into the old rocker and thoughts of the past.

After that night in the storm, Theodore got her work in the big house. Mostly cleaning and cooking. Although they carried on their affair under Miz Lucille's nose, they didn't begin to live together until after she passed away.

Vesta tried not to think about that unfortunate day, but today her mind had a mind of its own.

Surely Miz Lucille had known they were together, but in those days white women usually felt relief when husbands left them alone at night.

Vesta had her first baby, a boy she named Odean, and he looked like Theodore. The second child, whom they named Lee, looked more like Vesta's family; he was a squat and chubby baby with a reddish complexion. Twin boys, Thom and Preston, were finally followed by their only girl – Lila.

Many things could be said about what happened the day of the accident - the day Miz Lucille died. It just seemed that finally the women – and the man between them - had had enough of walking around the truth.

Odean and Lee had already been born. Vesta was pregnant with the twins and assigned to easy chores around the plantation.

One day Miz Lucille, perhaps feeling the heat of the oppressive southern summer, decided to get on Vesta for every little thing. Nothing she did was right and had to be redone at least twice. Theodore at first said nothing, but as the day wore on and the bickering continued, Vesta burst into tears as Miz Lucille sent her to the hen house for the second time.

The big house was plantation style, large upstairs with four bedrooms and a broad stairwell in the middle of the house. Now decades later, sitting on her porch in the afternoon sun, Vesta allowed herself to remember coming back from the hen house and finding Miz Lucille sprawled at the bottom of the steps.

Theodore told the sheriff and the children that she may have tripped and fell down the steps. Lee confirmed that he found her and ran to get Theodore. Half-truths still didn't make a whole truth.

Four years later, Theodore asked Vesta to marry him. Of course they had to keep it a secret; they couldn't even tell the children. In these parts, folks "took care" of "uppity niggers" who thought they were just as good as white people.

Oh, Theodore was respected and all, but marrying some nigger girl would have been too much for the decent white folks of Teluhci. So Theodore and Vesta took a trip to

Louisiana; he had friends arrange everything so it was legal. They never told anyone about the marriage, family or friends, it was just for them.

What Vesta didn't know until Theodore died several years later, after a bad winter left him with pneumonia, was that he also arranged to leave half of everything he owned to her and their children.

That's when the famine part of life caught up with her family.

Old Theodore had been specific in his will; the property should be divided between his three remaining white children, Buckley, Harley and Linda, and Vesta and his colored children. The Teluchi side was to go to his white children. The Vermosa side, also known as The Hollow, was to go to his Negro family.

When Theodore died his friends in Louisiana filed the will on Vesta's behalf, and within six months the local court found it legal. His white children, led by his oldest son Buck, contested and appealed the will. After three years of appeals that went to the State Supreme Court, the will was upheld.

Vesta and her family owned half of everything; that included the acres they once sharecropped.

But Vesta sensed trouble as soon as Theodore's friend from Louisiana wrote her about the will. Her parents long dead and an only child, she had cousins on her mother's side that lived in Virginia. She made a decision to send Lila, her youngest child, to live with them for a while.

She tried to convince Thom to join Lila in Virginia. The twins were 18, but Thom was special; slow as folks would say. Not retarded, Vesta was quick to point out, just slow. He refused to leave his family, and when his brothers backed him up, Vesta gave in and allowed him to stay.

At 24 years old, Odean was the oldest and seemed determined to remain single. Lee married a girl from New Market, Lou Ella, and moved her and her family to The Hollow. Thom's twin Preston was a hellcat who loved moonshine, music, dancing and courting every unmarried girl he met. It would be a time before he settled down with someone. Lila was the baby, still shy, although definitely her mother's daughter. She seemed most attached to her brother Lee. Vesta thought that for Lila, leaving him would be the hardest part of going to Virginia.

With Lila in Virginia when the trouble started, the family thought they could handle it. At first, they could handle the simple threats. Then, someone found Odean's still and broke all his jars and equipment and stole the moonshine.

Soon after that, Thom found the family cow, horse and mule poisoned in the barn.

The hardest hit came when the Klan burned down Lee's house.

Dressed in the traditional white sheets and hoods, the white men of Teluchi rode up to the house and threw torches onto the roof and through the windows. It was a miracle that Lee and his wife, Lou Ella, managed to escape. They ran out the back door into the woods and hid until the Klansmen rode away.

Billy, Lou Ella's older brother, died in the fire, leaving behind a wife and three children. He had stayed over for the evening after he and Lee came in from the fields. Dinner and a few glasses of home brew later, he fell asleep on the floor by the front room window. He never had a chance.

Lou Ella and Lee went to the sheriff's office the next day and reported the crime. The sheriff said he'd look into the matter.

*   *   *   *

"Miz Vesta! My, you sure do look comfortable." Clara, Lee's mother-in-law stepped on the porch and shook Vesta's shoulder gently.

"Oh, Clara . . . I'm sorry I didn't hear y'all come back," said Vesta as she woke up with a start. "I been napping all afternoon, and here it is past time I should have had these peas ready."

"Now don't you rouse yourself. We got time to get supper ready." Clara turned to watch as Lou Ella and Iona climbed the steps. "Here, let me take those peas. I'll go ahead and put them on and we'll get washed up and come back out and sit a spell with you before I start the cornbread." She took the bowl of peas and opened the screen door. "Iona will bring you a cool glass of water, won't you, baby?"

Vesta watched as three-year-old Iona skipped ahead; she and Clara disappeared into the house, leaving Lou standing on the porch.

"Lou, how you doing this evening?" Vesta asked her silent daughter-in-law.

Lou watched her mother and Iona chatter their way down the hall. Thin and hard-looking, wearing a limp and tattered field dress, Lou at only 22 looked like an old woman.

She had been 16 and beautiful when Lee married her and bought her and her family to The Hollow.

Her family helped sharecrop the land. Along with her parents Clara and Booker, she had two siblings, her older brother Billy Boy and Marie the youngest. When Theodore died and the property became Vesta's free and clear, Lee worked out a deal with them so they continued to live and work on the land.

A year after Billy's untimely death, 12 year-old Marie was raped and became pregnant. She died the night she gave birth to Iona.

Lou was also pregnant at the time, and next to her own expected baby, Marie was her heart and soul. She called her My and looked after her while Clara and Booker spent their days in the field.

The night Marie died, grief-stricken Lou Ella picked up the baby and announced to her mother and the midwife, "I own her now and she's mine." When they tried to take the baby from her she ran with the infant and hid out on the mountain.

A week later, after the search party had given up hope of finding them alive, Lou staggered into the yard of the family house carrying Iona. Her hair was almost gray, she was thin and dirty and her dress was torn and bloody. Somewhere, somehow, she had lost her unborn baby. The body would never be found.

She raised one hand and pointed her finger at the family as they rushed out to greet her.

"There is nothing but blood and death in this place," she said. She hadn't spoken a word since then.

Now, Lou walked up the steps and through the front door without acknowledging she had ever heard Vesta's greetings.

Vesta thought again of the time the Klan burned down Lee and Lou's house. They had first gone to live with her parents and Marie. Somehow things didn't work out there and after Thom was killed they moved in with Vesta.

"Thom," Vesta sighed. She thought she had finally been left with just the sweet memories of her son, but grieving his hideous death was still a sore spot.

He was so innocent. Someone so fine surely didn't deserve to die the way Thom did. She sighed again, and this time a pain slowly inched its way along her side.

It was a weekend. The men had been down at the juke joint woman's house when they heard about Thom.

The next day, Emma Jane, the juke joint woman, came to console her and tell all she knew about what happened.

After all these years she could still visualize his butchered body as though it were yesterday.

The pain in Vesta's right side had reached her heart and now exploded all through her body. She clutched her chest and attempted to rise from the rocking chair; midway up she collapsed and fell backward. Her eyes focused for the last time on The Hollow trail and she saw herself as a strong young woman again striding forward on the trail for the last time.

EJ'S STORY

Getting up was easy; gathering together last night's pain and anger took concentration and determination. The sorting out of personal insults and trying to remember all that happened made the floor under the wooden crate she used as a table, feel like the best place to spend eternity.

Emma Jane, EJ to friends, got up.

She surveyed the room. It was a mess. Last night's gathering had gotten out of hand - starting with the first drink. EJ did not drink with her customers. In fact, she did not usually drink at all. The constant stench of moonshine in her clothes and on her skin was enough to put her off whiskey for life.

She stepped over the outstretched body of Hap Turner. Wet-sounding snores told her he was alive.

She walked her graceful fat woman's walk through the large room toward the small back room that was her only private space in the juke joint she called home. She counted two more bodies. Her head throbbed like it was squeezed by large and calloused hands. She did not stop to see who the bodies belonged to, or if they were alive or dead.

The cracked and blurry mirror above the washstand told her that the intolerable hangover was not the only reason her head ached. A large bruise across her right cheekbone was both hot and tender when she touched it.

Surprise and memory flooded her face.

"Damn fool hit me," she hissed to the mirror.

A pitcher sat on the floor beside the washstand. She picked it up and poured water into a large tin bowl. She used a faded piece of rag to bath her bruised face.

Another glance in the mirror intensified the anger that now simmered below the surface like a pot of burnt beans.

Last night had started out like the usual Thursday night. Except for the regulars, business was slow. Hap, Charlie and Lee had been sitting around arguing about who should buy the next shot of whiskey. Hap, as usual the loudest, reminded the men that last month on a Sunday night he bought everyone in the house a drink after he got lucky in a crap game.

EJ had not been paying much attention. Her Thursday night chores weren't done yet. The small four-ounce Mason jars she used to serve the home brew were still soaking in a pan of soapy water. She stood in her kitchen over a hot wood burning stove frying chicken for the sandwiches she would sell later.

"EJ brang us another bottle, and put it on Lee's bill," Hap yelled from the front room.

EJ checked the chicken before reaching under the kitchen table for a bottle of Odean's white lightning. They were still arguing about who would pay for the drinks when she walked into the front room.

"Man, I swear you the biggest liar 'round this mountain." Lee held a tin cup to his mouth and drained the last drop. He wiped his lips with the back of one large callused hand.

"Alright, let's roll for it." Hap set his glass down on the wooden table EJ would wake up under in less than 12 hours.

"Hey, Charlie," Hap turned to the young man who stood by the door watching the last of the summer sun go down over the creek, "you brang your dice?"

"Sho' nuff, always keep my babies near and dear," Charlie said as he turned away from the doorway and put his hand in the breast pocket of his green and black short-sleeved work shirt.

As he strolled toward them, EJ mused that if only she were younger, and a lot less fat, she'd like to find out how he was between the sheets. Instead she yelled, "Y'all know I don't allow no gambling in my house."

"That's right EJ, don't let these trifling men gamble in your house!" Lee laughed his beer-belly laugh, head thrown back, mouth wide open.

Charlie and Hap weren't having any of it and had just decided to drag Lee out to the back porch for a friendly game when the door opened. Only Hap noticed Odean step inside and he turned to include the late comer in the familiar game of parting Lee from his liquor money.

Odean looked at the men and tried to speak but could not. Hap had never before seen him look this way. Something was wrong.

"They found him in Cullman County."

Lee had his back to the door and was still joking around when Odean spoke. EJ would never forget the way the light and life left his eyes. He had not even known his brother had entered the room, but he understood that Odean could only mean that Thom was dead in the Klan dominated Cullman County.

Thom had been missing for a few days. He was a slow thinking, gentle man who loved to fish. He also loved to gather the fruits, nuts and berries of the woodland surrounding their home for the women of The Hollow who would cook him a cobbler anytime he wanted. His family thought he was on one of his many excursions and would soon return with his usual bounty along with a request for cobbler or pie.

EJ saw Lee's cheek muscles relax; saw the fire in his eyes go out, and he looked at her and smiled an awful, toothy grin. She had known him for a long time, but at that moment, she saw something in him that scared her and she stepped away from him and shivered as if someone had walked over her grave.

He turned his solid body around to face Odean. His shoulders slumped and his steps were slow and deliberate as he stood up and walked to his brother. They gripped each other by the upper arms; Lee searched Odean's eyes. Together, they turned and went out into the treacherous southern night.

EJ watched them go, watched Charlie and Hap follow. She stood at the open door as they talked; impotent words of anger. When she smelled burning grease, she stepped back to the kitchen to remove the burnt chicken from the stove.

She knew it would have been easy to kill Thom. He had never developed defenses against the white world and had been well liked by everyone who met him, white or black. Except he was a Negro; he was also a Jamerson and a Ghee. The Ghee half was what had gotten him killed.

It had been six years since Theodore Jamerson died and left half of his property to Vesta and their children. The white half, led by Buck and Harley Jamerson, resorted to everything to run the Ghees off or scare them into selling the land.

Now, and for the second time, it seemed they had crossed the line with the murder of an innocent.

Later Hap came back to the juke joint and several of EJ's regulars stopped by, but none had yet heard that Thom had been found dead in a Cullman County ditch with a broken neck and his manhood missing.

That night the drinking had been hard.

EJ didn't remember when she started drinking. But she had, and she had lost control. Things turned ugly and Hap hit her.

She did remember that when Hap returned from going out after Odean and Lee, he bought a bottle of lightning and retreated to a dark corner of the porch to sit all alone in a

46

cane-bottom chair, one he made himself. To the first few people who asked him about the murder, he grunted only bare details. Finally, he refused to answer at all.

Later, before EJ lost control but after she had taken her first drink, Hap got some home brew - a sure sign he intended to do some serious drinking.

Now, EJ stood in the small back room, dressed except for her everyday head rag made from quilt scraps. She stood with one hand on a hip and tried to think around the fog in her still-aching head.

She remembered.

She had been dancing with a bad-news type from over Indian Creek way in Madison County. She started dancing with him to calm him down. When he came in and heard about Thom, he started talking about getting guns and going over to Buck's house and killing everyone. His ranting and raving started to stir everyone up, but EJ knew nothing could be done so she asked him to dance.

Hat Man, a blues player who came by from time to time to pick up some extra money, started playing something low and sad. She and the young man were doing a slow turn around the floor. She remembered him pressing her against the wall and trying to unbutton her dress.

Hap came to her rescue and there had been shouting and pushing. Whatever she said inflamed him so much that he hit her, and she fell to the floor and passed out.

Now, memory restored, she tied the head rag around her matted hair and went to see to whoever was passed out on her floor.

It was Slim Jim, a friend of Charlie's, and a woman she didn't recognize. They lay sprawled like rag dolls in heat on her dirty wooden floor. Both were dead drunk.

She would make strong chicory coffee, wake them, charge them a nickel a cup, and put them out. Friday was payday for many of her customers and she had a lot to do before she would be ready for the weekend crowd.

Unfortunately, Thom's death would be good for business. Drinking was all they had.

But first she decided, after she finished the necessary chores, she would go and pay her respects to the Ghee family.

LILA'S STORY

Mama's funeral took place on a bright and lovely day. Second Baptist's graveyard flowers all bloomed to say goodbye to mama. She would have loved seeing the flower petal heads nod in the unseasonable August breeze.

I wanted to hate the day for being so beautiful. Shouldn't funerals be on rainy, dreary days? After all, when you bury someone your heart's crying so why shouldn't the day reflect that? Still and all, Mama would have loved this day so I suppose I shouldn't begrudge her a beautiful home-going.

Old Pastor Crutcher delivered the eulogy. Mama and Old Pastor had known each other a long time. Some folks said he had once tried to court Mama back when she was a girl. Mama never allowed as to if that was true or not. She could keep a secret better than anyone I knew.

Mama hadn't even wanted to bother anyone with her death. Instead of calling out for help as she sat on the front porch in her old rocker, she just died. Miz Clara found her when she brought her a glass of water. When I returned home from the store that evening, she was gone; gone without saying a word to anyone, without saying a word to me.

Old Pastor sat with our family while his son made the final graveside remarks.

"Proverbs tells us that if we find a virtuous woman her price is above rubies; and y'all know Sister Vesta Ghee was

49

a mighty fine woman. Yes, Lawd, she was a woman who worked with her hands for the benefit of her family, and yes, Lawd, she also provided for those in need. Surely, surely her works will praise her through the gates of heaven."

Young Pastor Crutcher was a fine speaker. A high school graduate preaching since he was 12; he was a tall, dark as a blackberry, serious man. He'd been pastor of Second Baptist since Old Pastor retired last year. Mama would have been pleased to know he had the final remarks.

The time had come for me to say goodbye. Everyone wanted me to toss a handful of the red clay soil into the grave. I couldn't do it; I wouldn't do it! Tears ran down my face and I turned to my family to explain that since Mama hadn't said goodbye to me, I wasn't ready to say goodbye to her.

Everyone looked back at me. Odean, Preston and Lee waited patiently with wet faces; grown men grieving for Mama. Miz Clara and Preston's girlfriend, Mozell, looked at me with pity. Lou held Iona, who kept asking "Why is everyone crying?" It was too much.

I turned away from the raw Alabama earth that would soon hold my mother forever and ran off into the beautiful August afternoon.

*　　　　　*　　　　　*　　　　　*

Out of the corner of my eye I saw Ben Taylor's lanky frame slip into the store without a sound.

I bet he was up to one of his tricks. Ever since I'd known him, Ben was always funning around. At school he put a frog inside Miz Battle's desktop and when she opened the drawer it leaped out and landed on her head. He got a caning that day!

It didn't matter to Ben that we were now adults. He still loved to get into mischief. EJ told my brother Odean that last month Ben caught some boys swimming naked in the Chickamauga Creek and stole their clothes. They had to run for home naked as Blue Jays!

Lately Ben had been hanging around the store, and me. He said he wanted to "come by and sit a spell." Humph! I didn't need him to keep me company. I already had the store and my family. Since Mama passed away, I had to take responsibility for the household. Miz Clara couldn't do it all alone and my sister-in-law Lou never said a word, never cooked or cleaned up; it seemed like she only cared about Iona. So my brothers' needed me.

I already had responsibilities. I didn't need silly Ben to go adding anything else to my life. Besides, he was just a field hand.

Ben found me attractive, I guess. All my life folks had commented on how I looked. My skin was fair, and from Mama I had inherited silky, coarse hair. Her hair had been midnight black, like my grandfather, but my hair was copper, taking after my white papa's side of the family. I wore my hair long and men usually found it my best feature. I was tall for a woman. My brothers were all over six feet tall, except Lee who was the shortest. I also had Mama's round, black eyes. Folks told me they flashed when I was excited.

"Ben Taylor, I see you," I snapped at him without turning around. "You just stop your nonsense right now, you hear!"

"Well, I was goin' to surprise you with this, but I guess you think they ain't good enough for you," Ben said.

A wonderful smell overwhelmed me and I turned around to find him standing behind me holding out a large bouquet of jasmine, magnolias, honeysuckle and wild roses.

No one had ever picked flowers for me!

Ben rushed to put them in my arms. As I reached for them a thorn scraped its way up my hand and bit into my wrist. I gasped and dropped the lovely bouquet on the floor.

Ben's smile melted like butter in a hot skillet. His eyes went dark with anger. He clenched his fists, cords of muscles stood out along his arms, and a vein throbbed in his neck. He wasn't much taller than I was but at that moment he seemed to loom over me by 10 feet.

"I do all I can for you," he said as he pressed his hard, sweaty body against me. "You can't keep treating me like I don't matter!"

He grabbed me and crushed me in his arms. His face came closer and closer until our lips came together in hungry kisses. His hands roamed all over my body, and everywhere they touched it felt like fire.

Outside, the snorting of horses announced the arrival of a customer.

Ben reluctantly pulled away from me, smashing the wildflowers underfoot. I blamed their scent for making me feel so lightheaded.

"I'ma talk to Odean 'bout us getting married," Ben said, as he stood in the doorway blocking out the bright morning sun, grinning again as if I had already said yes. "You better start sewing a white dress."

I grabbed the closest thing to me and flung it at him as he ducked and ran outside laughing to beat the band!

All that week I waited for my brothers to say something about Ben. He had already spoken to Odean; Dora Thomas offered her congratulations when she stopped in the store Thursday to buy some bags of sugar, a jar of molasses and a sack of flour.

Dora's husband, Mosey, was Odean's friend. They saw each other often. Mosey usually helped Odean out with his moonshine still. Of course, his help usually involved a few free drinks.

Odean wasn't usually talkative. Unlike most moonshiners, he hardly ever sampled his own merchandise. Of course, like most men, he did drink. He just never let it interfere with business.

During the week I worked the store, allowing my brothers to do field work, feed and care for our animals, and pick up whatever we needed to stock the store.

On weekends the store was their territory. They claimed to work, but usually friends came by and they played cards, dice or checkers on the back steps. Odean sold shine or home brew out behind the store. Precious else was sold unless it was to strangers.

Saturday was wash day. I stood in the back yard stirring lye soap into hot well water. Fire licked the bottom of our huge cast-iron kettle. Around the yard lay four big piles of clothes ready for washing. Rambler, Preston's hound dog, sniffed around each pile searching for a treat.

I stood up to rest my back for a minute, and looked up at the sun. I had so much to do, but already it was noonday.

"Damn Lou, she never helps out with anything," I muttered as I bent over to put a pile of white clothes in the boiling water.

"Lou ain't at home?" Lee spoke behind me. I whirled around, nearly upsetting the wash kettle in my surprise. Lee grabbed my arm to help me keep my balance.

"Lee!" I said in surprise, "I didn't hear you come up behind me."

He held my arm and caressed it before letting go. He stood close to me with his arms folded across his chest. Lee was on the heavy side with a belly that shook when he laughed, which was often. One half of his round face was covered with stubble; he only shaved on Sundays. An old felt field hat slouched across his forehead.

"I come up 'round the side of the house. Lou ain't home?"

"No, she and Iona gone down to the spring. Iona wanted

to catch crawfish and Miz Clara gone over to visit a spell with Miz Jessie."

"Nobody else at home with you?" Lee asked.

"No," I answered and started putting the white clothes into the hot soapy water.

Lee looked off in the distance, over toward the mountain. When he looked back at me he seemed to inspect me for faults.

Odean was the older brother. He was a quiet man who seldom raised his voice, or found fault with much of anything. When I was younger, Odean was my savior. I ran to him when I wanted candy or needed to talk.

Preston was a teaser. Like Ben, he played every trick in the book. Preston introduced me to snuff, gave me my first taste of moonshine, and taught me how to ride a horse. He also explained where babies came from. His explanation scared me so badly that I remained a virgin even at 16.

Lee was the serious one, and after Papa died, Mama said Lee was in charge of our family. All my life I believed that. Lee made sure I did my schoolwork and chores and spanked me when I misbehaved. I loved Lee more than anyone else.

As Lee continued to inspect me I started to fidget, to straighten my skirt and smooth back my fly away hair. I didn't want him to find fault with me. Finally, he raised his eyes to mine.

"Ben done spoke for you," he said.

Now, it was out in the open.

"Well, what you got to say for yourself?" Lee raised his voice and unfolded his arms.

"I, uh, what do you think, Lee?" Had Lee found out about the kiss in the store? Did he know how I felt? The memory of that kiss made me feel so guilty.

Lee looked at me some more. He placed his hands inside the pockets of his faded overalls. Under his gaze I started to sweat. When he looked at me like this, it meant I was in trouble. I felt 10 years old again and about to get a licking.

"Let's go inside. I guess we need to talk." Lee turned and walked towards the back door.

All I could do was follow.

*   *   *   *

We all wore our Sunday best when Ben came to call.

Lee wanted to be sure I was married off proper. After all, I was the youngest and the only girl in the family. My brothers had decided that I would have a church wedding with all the trimmings. Ben had been instructed to make a formal propose before the entire family.

Sunday supper waited. Miz Clara and I had fixed fried chicken, fresh green beans from the garden, roasted sweet potatoes, sliced tomatoes and onions and cornbread. For dessert, Miz Clara had made her famous butter roll and I'd cooked a peach cobbler.

We all crowded into Mama's front parlor. The only one missing was Mama.

Lou, Miz Clara and I sat on matching pairs of faded, chintz-covered rosewood settees. The cabbage rose wallpaper was now discolored in spots, mostly around the front window, the wall and floor.

Preston and Lee waited over by the window; Lee in his favorite chair, the handmade cane-bottom rocker Mama was in when she died. Preston sat in a rosewood chair; the cushion was covered in the chintz fabric that matched the settees. Odean stood in a far corner, his hands folded across his chest.

Iona played house, rearranging Mama's whatnots, moving between the mahogany cabinet against the back wall to the small round table between the rocker and the chintz-covered chair to the large oval table that separated the settees.

We'd just come home from church, so we were already dressed for the occasion. The men in Sunday suits, we women in high-necked dresses with long puffed sleeves. The waist of my dress was too tight; I felt faint. Iona alone had been allowed to relax into a sturdy pink and white gingham jumper.

"Here he come," Odean was the first to spot Ben as he stepped off the trail and approached the house. "He look scared!"

"Now remember, we ain't gonna question the man to death," Lee said as he smoothed his jacket. "Odean and I already decided Lila should get married."

"Past time," Miz Clara said under her breath. "Lawdy, I sure do wish your mama would have lived to see this day."

Ben banged on the screen door and Preston got up to open the door. We all watched as Ben shuffled from foot to foot, crushing a soft hat between his large, bony hands.

"Uh, evening Miz Clara, Lou, Lee, Preston, Odean." Ben bobbed his head after each name. "You too, Iona."

"Ben," Iona ran to him and tugged on his jacket, "you got candy?"

Lou surprised everyone by rescuing Ben. She jumped up to take his hat and led Iona back to sit between her and Miz Clara on the settee. I'd never seen her look so alive. I watched her as she watched Ben. I was so caught up in the fire in her eyes and the flush on her face that I just about missed Ben stammer out the proposal.

"As y'all know, Lila and I been friends since we was little." Without his hat Ben had begun to wring his work-hardened hands together. "And, uh, uh, I had been in love with her a long time."

"Yes, yes," Preston was impatient and wanted to be off to his family down the mountain. He and Mozell had two young children now, and he'd just finished building the family a cabin. Preston was still a ladies man, but Mozell had done a good job of settling him.

Ben perspired into his starched shirt. He took a large white handkerchief out of his pocket and wiped his forehead, then shifted again from foot to foot.

"Y'all know me and you know I ain't got much. I still help my Daddy sharecrop over on the Burtons' property."

Everyone looked at Lee. Lee looked Ben over as if he'd never seen him.

"But I'ma hardworking man and I heard they hiring colored workers at the mill." Ben looked up with expectation at Lee. When Lee still didn't say anything, Ben stuck his hands in his back pockets and rocked back on his heels.

"I'm asking for Lila to be my wife." Ben's voice raised up a notch as he made his declaration but he finally seemed to relax.

"Well now, Ben you know Odean's the eldest, and it be his to say if we gone give our girl away," Lee said, leaning forward in his seat. "We know you to be a good man."

"Guess we gonna have a wedding." Odean was quick to end Ben's misery.

Everyone sighed with relief. Miz Clara started crying and going on about how Mama would have wanted to be here for this. Preston got up and pounded Ben on his back so hard the poor man started coughing. Iona danced around clapping her little hands. Lee and Odean shook Ben's hand and started asking him about the new mill just opened in Morgan County.

No one noticed as Lou came over to me, giving me a quick hug and an even quicker smile. I watched in open-mouth surprise as she went into the dining room and started setting out Mama's good china. I tried to remember the last time I'd seen her smile. I figured it had been before Iona was born; before her sister Marie died in childbirth.

Lou Ella Ghee hadn't smiled since she lost her mind and stopped talking!

It was as if she, along with everybody else, approved of my marriage to Ben.

When Truly was born I remembered again how Lou smiled, for the first time in a long time, when Ben Taylor came and proposed before the family.

Since that day, Lou seemed a changed woman, as if she'd awakened from a sleeping spell. A Negro Sleeping Beauty awake after a hundred years of slumber. Or like Ichabod Crane waking up under a tree after the nightmare of "Sleepy Hollow."

Still, Lou refused to talk.

She seemed happier; helping out with the housework, even coming into the store and doing whatever was asked of her. She started taking an interest again in her appearance, wearing clean clothes and combing her hair. Everyone was amazed at the change in her.

We thought it was only a matter of time till she spoke.

Ben and I married two weeks later; country people don't believe in or need long engagements. Miz Clara helped me sew my dress and Odean stood up with me as we said our vows before young Pastor Crutcher.

Four months later my brothers, Ben, and some friends built us a small cabin not far from the store. Lee said it was so that I didn't have to walk far to go to work. Ben said he didn't want his wife working, but it turned out a good thing that I kept my job in the store; not that it paid much.

We all now had homes along The Hollow. Anyone wanting to visit the Ghees first walked up past the store to Ben and my house. Preston's house was next; he and Mozell had two boys and a girl. Miz Clara's cabin was abandoned; after Mama died she moved in with Lee and Lou. They all lived in the family home at the top of the mountain.

Odean was the only one still not married. He never seemed that interested in women. Over the years many women had tried to tempt him, but when things seemed to be getting hot and heavy he'd simply take off for weeks at a time, never telling his current sweetheart when he'd return.

EJ had her eye on him. She was the only woman who never gave up on him.

EJ lived behind the store and up the mountain a ways. Mosey, Dora and their daughter, Betty, also lived in The Hollow; paying rent to my brothers for the cabin.

I never told anyone that I didn't love Ben. Lee decided it was time I married, and that was that.

On our wedding night Ben seemed surprised that I wasn't a virgin, but he never asked any questions. He was just happy that now I was in his bed every night.

That first night we made love he was gentle with me. I don't know what I expected but it was . . . different. The passion I felt when he held me in his arms that day in the store was gone. Ben spent a lot of time caressing me and telling me how beautiful I was.

When Miz Clara helped me make my wedding gown, over needle and thread, she told me that a wife should satisfy her husband's sexual demands. I took for granted that this was how a marriage would be.

Yet, I did want more. I tried to talk to Ben about what was wrong, but I was too embarrassed to let him know exactly what I expected. When I tried to show him, it was his turn to become embarrassed, and he told me that making love that way would surely hurt the baby.

Yes, I got pregnant right away. In fact, it must have been on our wedding night because Truly, who came early, was born exactly eight months later.

*   *   *   *

"Ben Taylor! Ben, you get your trifling self out of the house so I can get some cleaning done!"

"Why you always fussing at me, Lila?"

"Why you keep hanging 'round getting in my way?"

"Lila, you know I been cut off the line at work and its wintertime. There just ain't no other work available."

"Why don't you go help Lee out at the store?"

"Humph, they don't need no help."

"Well, it ain't like they doing hard labor down there now, is it?"

"Yeah, and that's what I mean. Why go down to the store when I can be with my baby and get me some lovin'?"

"Get away from me! I'm tired of you slobbering all over me!"

"What you mean, woman, you ain't never said that when you want it."

"When you think I want it, huh? You think I want it when you crawl in bed at night sweaty from the mill? Think I want it when I'm tired and you come shoving it in me every chance you get?"

"No, I guess you don't want it. I guess you want whoever it was took you 'fore I got there. Ain't that so?"

"He was a better man than you'll ever be!"

"Who, Lila, tell me who?"

"No, I ain't, and don't you ever ask me again, else I'ma take Truly and go back home."

"Oh, you gone go home, is you? First, you let some man take what shoulda been mine, now you gone run off and take my baby!"

"She mine!"

"What you sayin', woman? You say all them folks been right? Talking about how much Truly look like the Ghees, when what they want to say is that she don't look like me and mine!"

"You the one talking, saying things you gonna regret."

"You know I got some regrets, Lila. Talkin' ain't one of them."

"Where you going?"

"I need a drink and I need some time to think."

"Ben, you come back here! Ben you hear me!"

*　　　　　*　　　　　*　　　　　*

America was at war.

Funny thing, war. Men get all excited about rushing off to go kill other men they ain't never seen, who don't talk the same language, and just have to fight to defend their own country. But, maybe the foreign men just want to kill somebody as well.

This war was overseas on somebody else's land. The War Between the States was fought between South and North. Brother against brother; the South defending slavery,

64

the North trying to end it. At first I wondered if they had a slave problem overseas and wanted America to help them end it.

For the first time in my memory white men started coming into the store, buying things but mostly just hanging around trying to talk to all the field hands who'd come in after work. They talked about how colored men could go off and fight now that we was free. They said the Army offered to pay colored men same as they paid white men. And you got free food, clothes and shelter.

It wasn't talk about free food that got colored men in the Army. It was the talk of freedom. Oh, we fought a war to be free, but around here a colored man was still a slave. A few men like my brothers owned land but most were sharecroppers or worked at the mill when they could. Even when you owned land, you got less for your crop than what they give the white man.

It was talk of freedom that won them men. Soon three local men signed up to go. Lemon Crutcher, Pastor Crutcher's baby brother, called Lemon cause he had the lightest skin in his family, he went off first; Joey Williams and Lee Turner followed.

Then Ben and Preston signed up and our family became part of the war effort.

We were still on shaky ground since our fight. Ben would come home from whatever job he'd managed to get, wash up and have dinner with me and Truly. Sometimes he'd play with the baby, and sometimes he'd just stare at her. Those were the nights that often ended in him getting drunk and forcing me.

He'd usually start by telling me he would show me who was the boss and who was the better man and who was the man of this house.

His rough hands would grab me and throw me on the bed or against the wall where he would force himself on me.

He was so passionate; at least he wasn't ignoring me, but the next morning he was always sorry. He'd apologize over and over again and talk about how he didn't mean to hurt me. I never told him that those were the only times I enjoyed pleasuring him.

The morning they left, Mozell and I both wept; Mozell, because now she'd have to take care of the boys without a father. Preston Jr. and Jacob were a wild handful. Willa was a good girl, but still too young to be of much help. Mozell had also just learned that she was pregnant again.

I cried because I thought I'd finally come to love Ben.

July 22, 1919

It is with deep regret that the United States Department of the Army must inform you of the death, in the line of duty, of Private Ben Taylor.

July 22, 1919

It is with deep regret that the United States Department of the Army must inform you of the death, in the line of duty, of Private Preston Ghee.

"It ain't decent! Fishin' on Sunday just ain't right. Humph!" Dora said, resisting our pleas. "Sunday is the Lord's Day."

EJ, Mozell and I gathered in Dora's kitchen, sipping chicory coffee while we tried to get Dora to come down to the fishing hole. Truly scrambled between our legs and the chair legs playing hide and seek.

"Well, the Lord wants us to go fishin' today," said Mozell as she sipped a cup of the strong brew. Her plump body filled out an old field shirt that had been one of Preston's favorite. A pair of faded jeans and air conditioned brogans completed her outfit.

"Yep, the Lord done told me that he wants a mess of fried perch for supper tonight," added EJ as she bent to pick up Truly. The treasures under the table continued to tempt the three year old and she whimpered and squirmed in EJ's arms.

"Alright, you only want to come to me when you want something I got," EJ said and released Truly to the dust bunnies. "I'll remember that next time I bake cookies!"

"Scripture says we must honor the Lord's Day and keep it holy," Dora was not easily led astray. She took a tray with fresh biscuits from the squat, black cast iron, wood burning stove and placed them on a wooden board to cool.

"Well, I ain't asking you to come down to my place and dance naked on a table top," EJ said, building up a full steam of choice expressions to tell Dora when she noticed Mozell giving her a "be quiet" look.

Grumbling, EJ reached for a hot biscuit, which she broke open, poured molasses over each piece and took a big bite from one. She was dressed in a faded gingham print house dress with torn off sleeves, mismatched buttons and a torn hem. Her large breasts threatened to pop through the thin fabric with each bite she took.

"You didn't go to church today, did you?" Mozell asked Dora. It was a sly question because we already knew she hadn't and why. Her husband Mosey, Odean's best friend, had gone out drinking last night and ran the wagon into a rut and broke off a wheel. Dora gave him hell and he'd gone off to find a spare part and he still hadn't come home.

"Now you know good and well services today were held over in Lacey Springs," she faced us with hands on hips, lips poked out and a watch out expression on her face.

"Now, now, we didn't come to start no mess, Dora," time to make peace I thought, "but we going fishin' and we thought maybe you'd like to come."

EJ and Mozell held their breaths. If anybody could talk Dora into something, they thought, it would be Lila.

I was tired and just wanted to get to the riverbank and catch fish. Truly was so active now; she kept me on my feet running after her all the time.

Dora still hesitated. She walked over to the doorway and stood, back to the group, looking out at the mountain. It was a pleasant day, she thought, and it wasn't like she had intended to do anything important. Turning back to the women, she said, "OK, just let me wake up Betty and tell her we going fishin' and I'll be back in time to fix supper."

Sixteen-year-old Betty was Mosey and Dora's only child and spoiled rotten. It was nearly 10 o'clock and she was still in bed.

EJ and Mozell smiled and relaxed. We all started to talk about the fish and who would most likely catch the most or the biggest.

I bent over, picked up Truly, placed her on my knee and bounced her at a rapid pace while singing her favorite ditty.

"Mama's little baby love shortenin', shortenin', mama's little baby love shortenin' bread. Bring on the butter, bring on the jam, cause mama's little baby love shortenin' bread."

Finally we left Dora's tin-roofed house and headed toward the river. Dora's house was on the right-hand side of the trail close to the river but we still had to walk downhill about a mile.

Single file we went down to the river bank. We checked spot after spot, debating the area's short comings and best features. One area was grassy; another area was not large enough to provide comfort for a foursome.

Several times I stopped to look back over my shoulder, the other women noticed but only EJ knew why.

Mozell found the perfect spot. It was a huge area with a shady Elm tree under which Truly, who was now fast asleep, could continue her nap. On the right side, bamboo grew high and sturdy. A huge boulder rose from the muddy river on the left-hand side.

The boulder rose from the bank seven or nine feet. It was flat topped and you could climb up on it and fish. Problem was it was so high up, the bamboo and sugar cane poles couldn't be let down into the water. No, the thing to do was go down the bank to a natural cove and fish.

Truly was getting too big for me to carry. Plus, she was so active. She often got into the strangest things. I laid her down with relief on the quilt Mozell spread out under an Elm tree. EJ placed our lunch, moon pies, crackers and a stick of bologna from the store - on the quilt. We had lemonade to drink when we got thirsty.

Dora and EJ had sugarcane poles with homemade cork bobbers. Mozell's bamboo poles had red and white striped plastic bobbers.

I had a pole and a rod and reel. Lee gave the rod to me for my birthday last year. I unraveled the line and checked for knots, liking the clicking sound it made when I cranked the line back onto the spool. "Lila, we come to fish," grumbled EJ, "not to admire that toy."

"It ain't a toy, 'sides I'll catch more with this than all the fish y'all gonna catch with those cane poles," laughing I turned to cast my line out into the muddy water.

"That a fact?" questioned Mozell.

"Yep, it is!"

"Sounds like a bet to me and I got a dollar say you wrong," EJ stood with her hands on ample hips. A red head rag covered her head and perspiration stood out on her forehead like greasy drops of water.

We discussed the bet and settled down for serious fishing. Mozell and Dora wanted to bet against EJ, but pride made them bet against Lila. Mozell only had fifty cents to bet so they fussed over the reduced price until Dora got the first bite.

Dora found shade by the side of the boulder and threw her line out in the shallow area. Delicious, but small, perch loved to hide and feed in a shady spot. Dora had one eye on her cork, as she listened to the women's banter, when she saw the first nibble. That's all it was, a nibble so small the cork barely floated from side to side. She waited two or three more nibbles and the cork was pulled under the surface of the water.

With one hand she pulled up and back on the cane pole.

"Well, you ain't gonna win no bet with that baby," I laughed at the small fish that dangled from Dora's hook. I stood up and looked around several times, "speaking of babies, I'ma go check on Truly," I said and turned away to walk back up the hillside.

"We not betting on the size, Lila," Dora yelled behind me, "it's how many caught and this one's a keeper."

Dora left her pole lying on the ground by the boulder to put her catch in the piece of netting used to store the fish. She carried the light burden down to the river, threw the netting into the water and secured it by sticking the hooked handle into the mud.

Dora removed the straw hat she wore and wiped her forehead with the back of Mosey's dark blue work shirt. She bent over and lifted the jar of lemonade from a hole covered with water to keep it cool. She took a deep drink from the dripping jar.

"Whew, hard work like that sure does make a body thirsty," EJ joked. She and Mozell laughed at the small fish Dora caught causing such hard work.

Walking back up the bank, Dora stopped and asked EJ what had been on her mind all day. "Why do Lila keep lookin' over her shoulder?"

"You ain't heard?" questioned EJ.

"Heard what?" asked Mozell.

"Dora askin' why Lila so jumpy," EJ said.

"Yeah, she is actin' kind of nervous," Mozell said as she slapped away a few lazy flies.

"Y'all know Lou been off her rocker again."

"It's been over a year now since Ben and Preston been gone."

"Been longer, started after Truly was born."

"Oh, now I remember how strange Lou acted that night. Looking at that baby like she seen a ghost."

"Don't you remember how she grabbed Lila by the arm and got all up in her face?"

"Sure do, midwife shooed her out, but not before she'd left a mark on Lila's arm; high yeller do bruise easy."

"But, why?" asked Dora.

"Don't know, but somethin' wrong. Lou is watchin' Lila all the time. Lila 'fraid she might hurt Truly," EJ glanced around, "and that's all I know."

"All you know or all you gonna say!" Dora and Mozell pestered her but she folded her arms across her ample chest and wouldn't say another word.

When I returned I announced that Truly slept the sleep of babies and fools. We traded comments good naturedly about each other's fishing abilities and went back to waiting for supper to bite.

Morning moved to afternoon; the sun shifted from east to north. Fishing proved fruitful. EJ caught a mess of catfish. In addition to the original small perch, Dora now had five others to join the school.

Mozell had carp, buffalo and perch.

As expected, I caught the most fish. The dark blue rod flashed in the water often. Bass, buffalo, cat and good sized perch rested at the bottom of my net.

I had chosen a shady spot near the bamboo, but now that the shade was gone I stood up and went back up the hill to check on Truly, asleep on the quilt, one more time.

"Oh no, Truly's gone!" In a panic I raced around calling for my baby. EJ and Mozell got up to help look for Truly.

Sitting by the boulder, Dora caught what she thought was her big catch of the day. She had been watching the cork bobber do a sideways dance for a few minutes. When finally the cork went under she grabbed her pole and pulled it up and backwards. She was so delighted to feel such a heavy weight on her pole, she didn't realize Truly had gone missing.

"Come out, Truly, come to mama, baby, come here." I was yelling and crying at the same time.

The thing at the end of Dora's line fought like no fish she'd ever caught. The cane pole bent pulling the line underwater. Dora stood up, jerking the pole towards her. At first she thought she'd lost the fish until the line came out of the water, seeming to go on forever, water droplets sparkling like diamonds in the sun. In the few second before the line reached Dora it moved, squirmed and wriggled. In horror she recognized the coils of a snake.

Thinking only of her safety, Dora flung the pole, line, bobber and all over her head. Her aim was good, the snake landed on the flat-topped boulder. Truly had discovered the sunny spot and played there with a rag doll.

Dora watched in horror as the snake landed on top of the boulder, its scaly body writhing as if in pain as it struck at the baby again and again.

After Truly died, grief led me to do something that only the men of The Hollow practiced. In private, I'd have a drink; only EJ and Mozell suspected how many drinks. Only they knew that sometimes I drank so much I'd pass out in the woods at night; crying for my lost baby and Ben, and for myself.

Odean showed me how to make home brew when EJ stopped selling or giving me the occasional bottle. It was funny, but I started to like making the bitter brew. Soon I added my own touches to the recipe Odean followed. He joked that I was a born 'shiner. Neither one of us could foretell how much this ability would serve the family in the future.

Miz Clara passed away and when her mother died, Lou seemed to mellow out once again. Strange as it seemed, we became friends. We found common ground in Iona.

Iona visited often and I found comfort in the talkative girl, she was my salvation in a way. Her chatter smoothed me in a way the shine never could.

Lou would come with her, of course. She never let the child out of her sight. But since Lou still didn't talk, Iona and I would spend the time talking to each other. Lou would position herself in the background watching, sometimes sewing, most often just sitting and rocking.

My relationship with Lee became strained. He came by to visit once, after Ben joined the army. We had words. I told him that he was no longer the man of my family. I never regretted the decision not to give him dominance over my life once again, even though Ben was gone.

Lee pointed out that without a husband I'd need his protection once again. I told him to leave. But before he left he told me something about my mother that shocked me. I wasn't surprised by the burden that he placed on my shoulders. It kind of explained everything about our parents. For the moment I just added it to the other secrets I harbored.

Now that Truly was gone, I was lonely, but in spite of that I never considered moving back in with my brother's family.

I did hunger for more children so I decided to marry once again and initiated a process of choosing a potential suitor.

At first I didn't find anyone I thought I could settle down with. The men who came into the store or who attended churches in the area were married already or no good skirt chasers. Farmers, sharecroppers or laborers – I'd already had one of that kind and didn't want another one. This time I wasn't going to let my family choose my man.

I still looked good; I had never worked hard like most country women. Working in the store, instead of field work, had helped keep me looking good. Neither had age dimmed it, like it had Mozell. Age and grief had given me a maturity and confidence that most men found disturbing.

One winter afternoon I had just sold some bags of feed to a local farmer when I noticed a stranger out back playing a game of dice with my brothers and the usual hanger on friends. He was a looker and dressed well, which was unusual for men around these parts. I moved to get a closer look. He spoke like an educated man and I determined to find out more about him.

His name was Mitchell Black and he was second cousin to Hap Turner. He worked as a railroad porter for the L&N Railroad. His life usually consisted of four months on the road and two months off the road.

Mitchell wasn't the marrying kind, but Lila looked good plus she had property, a business and no children. He had never went out with women of her caliber or known women who had a mind about things besides how they looked and what he could do for them.

With Lila he found conversation. She didn't know much current news but was eager to hear about government issues, wanted to know how Negros were treated in the North and what were his plans for the future. Lila stimulated something more than just his manhood.

They only had a two month courtship but Lila worked magic on him. He found that he not only wanted to keep seeing her, but that he wanted her to promise herself to only him. She said no, that she'd only give her promises to her husband.

That winter, before he returned to Chattanooga, Tennessee to begin his shift, they got married.

*   *   *   *

In the fall of 1923, revenuers paid a visit to The Hollow. It had never been a secret that Odean Ghee made the best shine in Morgan County. What was not so well known was that Odean had competition. The Fortney Brothers from Sumner wanted to control the market share of white lightning in the county. The brothers were white; Odean was colored.

Peter Fortney and Sheriff Moores went to school together and bonded as high school football big men. The Moores family owned the major share of the property in the county and had relatives in high places. While Howard Moores, "Howie" to friends, went into law enforcement, the Fortney bothers worked their father's property and supplied drink to the good citizens of Morgan and Cullman counties.

It didn't take long for the sheriff, the brothers and their friends to scout out Odean's still location. They posted a guard and the next time he showed up, he was arrested.

Moonshiners, colored included, usually got away with a small fine or paid a bribe to the authorities. With the connections the Moores had at the courthouse and beyond, Odean never stood a chance. He was sentenced to 10 years. He immediately started hard labor on the chain gang operating out of the Decatur jail.

Although the Ghee family was afraid for Odean and tried everything they could to get him out, they realized it could have been worse. He could have been sentenced to the prison in Cullman, and not many Negroes ever got out of that place alive.

Taking advantage of the Ghee misfortune, Buck Jamerson made sure government officials got alerted about the country store that Odean and his brother Lee owned. The long arm of the law reached out and appropriated the store and contents for back money owed the government for illegal sale of whiskey.

Lee had to sell off 20 acres to pay off the court fees and other fines imposed by the court just for good measure. An Englishman named Pitney had cattle to graze and the undeveloped area was perfect for him. Since he wasn't a local man, he did not have an allegiance with the Jamersons. Much as Buck schemed to get the property, it never came to be.

Without the influence of his older brother and the prestige of owning the store, Lee lost interest in farming and keeping up the property. He didn't appear to care about much of anything anymore. Drinking and running after women became his main occupation.

He no longer collected rent from the few families who lived in The Hollow. Since Lila didn't have the store to work in anymore, she took over those duties as well as other decisions about upkeep and maintenance. People seemed to like dealing with her better anyway, particularly the women.

Lou and Lee had never been much of a married couple. Everybody use to say how good he was to stay with a woman who wouldn't speak, who didn't take care of his needs and who often didn't take care of herself. Now those same folks talked about what a shame it was that he'd moved another woman into the cabin Miz Clara lived in when she was alive, right under his wife's nose.

It seemed as if Lou didn't mind at all.

Section Two

IONA'S STORY

Talking to Auntie Lou was easy.

Everyone else acted like she was deaf and dumb. But she could talk! That was our little secret. Sometimes she'd whisper things to me when I went to bed. The first time it happened she made me promise not to tell anyone, else she'd never speak to me again.

So I never did tell, at least not for a long time.

Auntie Lou was always with me. When I asked her why, she said she was my angel and that she'd made a promise to protect me because she'd failed to protect her little sister.

That was my mother. Auntie called her My, like a nickname, but her real name was Marie. She'd died when I was born. Grandma Clara told me that they'd never known who my father was, but one night when Auntie decided to talk she whispered to me that someone did know who he was.

I got all excited. I wanted to know! I pestered Auntie Lou for a long time after that, but she'd gone back to not talking and never mentioned it again.

But somehow it was OK; I had a big family. My uncles all took turns, when Auntie let them, teaching me all I'd ever need to know about chores and school stuff. Uncle Odean even taught me how to shoot a gun!

I had Auntie Lou, Aunt Lila, Granny, and Aunt Mozell and my cousins, baby Truly, Willa and those bad boys Junior, Jacob and Luther.

My cousin Willa was my best ever friend!

I was the oldest so she had to do what I said. We often played the store game and I was Auntie Lila; I made Willa be Uncle Ben. I'd be boss and tell Willa what to do. Granny caught us once; Willa was sweeping the floor while I fussed at her that she never did anything right. Granny laughed but she also said that we were making fun of folks and it wasn't a polite thing to do.

I understood, but Willa was only a baby and didn't know the difference anyway.

We had the best ever time in the summers!

Sometimes we all went exploring! Me, Junior, Jacob and Willa would go far up the trail, behind our house. We'd stand at the top of the mountain and look down on all the white folks on the other side. Up on that mountain we imagined that we were just as good as any of them. Of course we could only see the road and an occasional wagon or somebody riding a horse.

I loved to play at the river! We caught craw daddies in the streams that led away from the river and they were so funny to watch! They moved sideways and just when you thought they would not bite they would rush forward and bite on the fishing line.

You had to be patient with craw daddies but if you caught enough, Aunt Mozell would make gumbo, the best ever food in the world. Well, maybe second best. My favorite food was ice cream, something we got only on special occasions!

Junior was always interested in Uncle Odean's still. At least once every summer he'd insist on us all going to take a look. I was the oldest, but the boys always stuck together. That only left me and Willa. Times like that, I'd wish Truly was old enough to be part of our group.

So Willa and I'd tag along with them. Usually we never found anything of interest anyway, just a collection of kettles, big old pots, jugs and Mason jars. Uncle Odean moved it every other year anyway, and we'd have to look all over the mountain before we found it.

Once we found a jug with some of the liquid grown folks called shine or white lightening. Junior dared me to take a taste. I dared him back. And it went on like that for a long time. Finally Junior took a big gulp and made a yucky face. He started to breathe hard and his face turned a funny color and he threw up his breakfast.

We all screamed and we ran as fast as we could back to the barn. Junior laid down in the shade and took a long nap.

Junior pleaded with us not to tell anyone what happened, but that night I told Auntie Lou. For the first time in a long time she spoke to me and said that I must always tell if any one of us was sick or hurt; especially if anything happen to me. Auntie was serious; she held my arm and squeezed it tight. She made me promise that I'd always tell her if anything happened to hurt me, if anyone ever hurt me. I promised.

Besides, they never let us go far anyway before someone came looking for us. Usually that'd be Auntie Lou. That was OK.

I was the oldest, so I started school first. It all started out OK, except getting up so early in the morning. Uncle Odean laughed at me, he said the older I got the more I'd have to get up early, to do chores. When I asked if doing chores meant I'd get out of going to school he laughed even harder.

Getting up early wasn't all either. I had to walk to the schoolhouse, which was all the way down to the church. It was so far away. When we went to church on Sunday, one of my uncles drove the wagon and it didn't take so long.

I had to walk past the store and down Oat Sharp Road, which was away from where my family all lived. It was the farthest I'd ever walked. But I wasn't scared because Auntie Lou always walked with me, and walked me back too.

Other boys and girls also walked to school. I had never seen so many children before, even at church services. Some were OK, and some I hated.

I hated Seth Rogers. My first day at school he tripped me and everyone laughed. I fell down and my dress flew up around my waist and everyone saw my underwear. I had two dresses Grandma Clara made for me to wear to school; this one was pink with ruffles and I'd gotten it dirty already. I ran crying and told our first grade teacher, Miz Battle. She punished him and made him sit in the corner for the rest of the day.

That night Auntie Lou asked me how was school and I told her all about mean ole Seth Rogers. I also told her about the numbers we had to learn. I asked her why. But again she'd gone back to not talking.

Every day Seth did something else to me; not enough to get sent back to the corner again, but he'd do dumb things like trying to scare me by jumping out from around a corner or he'd steal my dinner bucket. Well, I kinda got use to it. Uncle Ben said that when a boy did dumb stuff like that it meant he liked the girl.

Well, I didn't like him!

That next Sunday at church, Auntie Lou walked over to Seth and hit him with her pocketbook. Bam, right on his big head. Boy, his mama wanted to fight there in church. She screamed and yelled at Auntie Lou, calling her crazy lady and other stuff. Of course

Auntie Lou never said anything back. She just stared at Seth's mama, daring her to do anything!

I tried to explain to Miz Rogers how mean Seth was to me at school. Miz Battle eventually got the story told and everyone calmed down but Auntie continued to give Seth and his mama the evil eye. Pastor's sermon that day talked about loving thy neighbor. Huh, what if they weren't the loving kind, I wanted to know.

Junior got to go to school the next year. After that, one after the other, Jacob, Willa and Luther joined us. So, I had all my cousins with me, but I was still the oldest and I still told them what to do.

Along about the time Willa started school, the children started asking me how come we all had the same last name if we didn't have the same daddy. Well that was a mystery. When I got home that night I reminded Auntie Lou she said someone did know about my daddy, but she just hugged me and wouldn't say.

So, I had no answer for the children. Once again, things turned mean. They started teasing me about not having a daddy. I did have a daddy but still it made me cry and Willa and Jacob cried along with me but Junior said he'd whip anybody who didn't leave me alone.

Junior made me so proud! He was the best ever cousin I ever had!

Uncle Ben and Uncle Preston went to war.

In class one day Miz Battle showed us on the map the place the men were fighting. It was hard to believe it was on the other side of the world. I raised my hand and said it was as far away as the moon. Miz Battle said the moon didn't have oxygen and she explained that oxygen was like air, something we needed to live.

They never came back from the war on the other side of the world so maybe they ran out of oxygen over there after all.

That's when I found out about death. My uncles didn't come back from the war and Baby Truly died and so did Grandma.

Grandma's death reminded me of when Nana died. Nana died on the front porch, shelling peas, sitting in the old rocker with the scarred up legs where cats sharpened their claws.

Grandma and I went to get her a glass of water and when we got back her head was back against the rocker, like she was sleep, but her mouth was opened.

I remember thinking that she looked kinda surprised.

When grandma died she was in bed. I wasn't supposed to look but when I peeked in her room, she had a surprised look on her face too. Made me think that death was a thing that snuck up on you; seemed that one day it would just tap you on the shoulder and you'd think "Oh, is it my turn?"

Nasty white men came and took Uncle Odean away. I thought it meant he'd die soon as well but Auntie Lou let me know that Uncle Odean wasn't dead, just sent away to some place called the prison. It sounded as deadly as war.

The white men also busted up Uncle Odean's still. Junior said that when he grew up he'd build it back again. I reminded him of how sick he got when he tried drinking the stuff and he said that when he was a man, he could drink anything!

I couldn't imagine him all grown up. He was all skinny, scarred up legs, buck toothed and clumsy as a colt. Had a piece of hair that stood up in the back of his head. Auntie Lila called it a cow's lick. That sent us all into giggles. Imaging a cow licking the back of Junior's head sure was funny!

Auntie Lou started to let me go visit Aunt Lila. She told me she thought I needed someone I could talk too. I tried to tell her that talking to her was all I needed. But she was right as always, because Aunt Lila needed me and I would soon need her too.

Aunt Lila married again. I could see why she loved him; Uncle Mitchell was the handsomest man ever! Only thing, he was gone for months at a time. One day they got married and he was gone. Didn't come back neither for almost a whole year.

Next time he left, Aunt Lila said she would soon have another baby. I was so excited! It just had to be another girl! Willa and me needed another girl in the family now that Truly was gone. Aunt Mozell worked in the city and wasn't home much and those boys were running wild. Auntie Lou and Aunt Lila took care of all of us.

Of course, I was still the oldest. Now, just as Uncle Odean promised, I had chores, like feeding the chickens and slopping the hogs and helping with the wash. And he was right, I didn't like it much!

One day I realized that I was just as tall as Auntie Lou.

My body was all of a sudden out of control. Sometimes I was sad and I didn't know why and sometimes I was happy and I didn't know why – I was confused.

Junior and Jacob started laughing at what they called the bumps on my chest. Willa wanted to know if they hurt. The boys at school started acting even dumber. Ole Seth Rogers got up enough courage to try and kiss me! Funny thing was, I kind of liked it, but I smacked him anyway so he'd know not to try it again.

I needed to talk to Aunt Lila but Uncle Mitchell was home from the train he worked on and they were together all the time.

Auntie Lou tried explaining what was happening, but her words got all mixed up and she stopped talking again. She got all mad about something that happened between men and women when girls grew up, and I didn't understand why.

One summer day, I went exploring with Willa and Luther. We had to babysit Luther 'cause he was still the baby after all. Junior and Jacob didn't join us exploring anymore, they said it was for babies. Now that we were all older, they had other friends they played with; boys just as bad as they were.

Me and Willa walked down to the road to take a look at our old store. It had been closed up a long time and inside it was dusty. Old boxes and bottles lay around on the floor, and the counter leaned to one side. Huge spider webs draped the ceiling like old lace clothes. All of a sudden, me and Willa was afraid of spiders. We dragged Luther out of there real quick.

We took an old path back up The Hollow thinking we'd visit Miz Dora and find out if Betty had come back for a visit. Betty was older than I was, but not as old as my aunts. She courted men and hung out at Honkey Tonks. She had a lot of great stories to tell about her friends and what went on in the city.

Walking up the path we ran into Uncle Lee. Ever since he lost the store, he'd been different. He looked different and he didn't stay at home anymore. It'd been a long time since I'd seen him. Aunt Lila said he had another family now, even though he was still married to Auntie Lou.

Uncle Lee was just as surprised as we were! He asked, "Where y'all going?"

"Going to visit Miz Dora," I said.

"Oh, Dora and Mosey ain't at home" he said.

"Did Betty come home for a visit?"

"Naw, Betty ain't been by visiting in a spell."

We talk on for a minute till he kind of tenses up and ask about Auntie Lou.

"She at home fixing supper," I said. "We'd better be getting back." Luther and Willa run off into the woods after that.

I noticed him looking at me kind of funny, looking up and down. It reminded me of the way the boys at school had taken to staring. I got that confused feeling again.

Finally he said, "You all grown up, Iona, you lookin' good."

He reached out to me and I backed away.

"I gotta get home now, Uncle Lee, but it was good to see you again." I quickly turned and ran after Willa and Luther.

Once I looked back over my shoulder; Uncle Lee stood there with his hands in the front pocket of his overalls, looking after me. He still had that funny look on his face.

"Aunt Lila, can I talk to you for a while?"

"Sure, Iona. What's on your mind?"

"Well... I don't know."

"Don't know?"

"Yea, I know what I want to say, but don't know how to say it."

"Well, everythin' got a beginnin' and an end. Try starting at the beginnin'."

"Oh, I can't go that far back."

"Alright, how about somewhere in the middle."

"Well... I been growing real fast lately."

"Mmm."

"And . . . things have been changing on my body. And growing!"

"Oh."

"Well, boys have been looking at me kinda funny! And they tease me too."

"Baby, you know how silly boys can be."

"Yesum."

"Should we talk more about what's happening to your body?"

"Yesum."

"It's going to be alright; you starting to become a woman."

"You mean I gotta have a baby!"

"No, no, Iona. It don't happen like that! It should take a long time for that to happen."

"Oh."

"First, things happen just like you noticin'. Your body starts to change."

"You mean like growing taller?"

"Yes, just so. First girls start to get a little taller than boys they same age. And girls start to develop breasts. You start growin' any hair under your arms yet, or anywhere else?"

"Yesum, the hair alright, but what about these breasts, when do they stop growing?"

"I think it depends on the girl. You know Sue Mae and Rema at church? Well, they the same age, ain't they? Sue Mae breasts are kinda big, just like her mama and her older sister. But Rema got small ones and I think hers done stopped growin'."

"Oh, so I won't know how big mine gone get till they decide to stop growing?"

"Yea, that's right."

"Oh. How long that gonna take, Aunt Lila?"

"Well, I think you should be all grown up in about another two years, so about when you turn 15."

"But that's too long!"

"Well, some other things gone happen as well."

"What!"

"You'll soon start havin' a monthly."

"Monthly what?"

"Now, this may be somethin' you can't understand now, Iona, but women have a natural habit of bleedin' every month."

"Natural! Bleeding!"

"Yea, baby. Listen to what I say first before you get all excited. Don't be afraid. One day you'll start feelin' kinda bad. You may have a fever, or stomach ache. Finally you think you got to pee, but when you go to the outhouse you'll see some blood coming from down there."

"Oh no, will it be a lot, will it come out fast, will it…"

"Hold on, I ain't finished yet. Now, like I say, there'll be blood. No, it won't come out fast, but it will come for several days, maybe even a week. But it will stop. After that it'll happen every month."

"Will it hurt?"

"Now, baby, don't cry. It's just a part of becomin' a woman. All women go through this till they get old."

"But what will I do? How will I stop it?"

95

"You gotta start getting' some rags together. Don't worry. I'll show you how and remember, when it happens come to me or Auntie Lou."

"Alright, but I ain't gonna like it!"

Aunt Lila said she'd need to talk to me some more after she had a talk with Auntie Lou first. But the baby came the next day!

They let me watch! Willa was so mad! She didn't get to watch because I was still the oldest!

Miz Dora came down from the mountain to help.

Auntie Lou kept wiping sweat off Aunt Lila's forehead with a cool rag. Miz Jessie, the midwife, kept me busy boiling water, fixing up the crib, fetching clean rags. Later I helped Miz Dora wash the soiled ones. It was hard work.

Aunt Lila was in a lot of pain. Sweat seemed to pour off her body, even though it was wintertime. She moaned an awful lot and when it was time for the baby to come she screamed louder than I ever heard anybody scream!

I'd seen the cow have a calf before so I knew what to expect. But when I saw the head come out between Aunt Lila's legs I stood in the corner and couldn't say a word. Miz Jessie grabbed the slippery baby and cut something with a pair of sewing scissors before she put the baby on a sheet held out by Miz Dora.

It was truly a miracle! It was a boy!

He started to cry. I started to cry! Everyone laughed and Miz Jessie told Aunt Lila it was a boy. She relaxes on the bed with a deep sigh and Auntie Lou and the midwife start pushing on her stomach. She started moaning again and I thought that maybe she was going to have another baby.

Miz Dora asked me to come help wash him. His little arms and legs waved wildly about, and he had a long navel. He was mad about something, he kept screaming as if he'd had to do all the work! After we finished washing him off, Miz Dora gave him to me to hold and rock till Aunt Lila was ready to feed him. He was so perfect! I counted the toes and fingers and when I put my finger in his mouth he started sucking it real hard. When I pulled it out, that got him mad again and he commenced to screaming all over again. I was sure everyone in The Hollow could hear him!

Aunt Lila name him Early.

The next day I told Willa and Luther all about the new baby. They don't believe me when I say how babies get born till I remind them about the cow. We all make gagging sounds!

So, Aunt Lila and I never got around to having the rest of that talk. At least not right away.

Winter that year was mean cold. Everything was extra hard. Auntie Lou and me had a lot of work to do. Uncle Lee or Uncle Odean used to do all the wood chopping and most of the water hauling. Now we had to do everything.

Sometimes Mr. Mosey and Mr. Hap would come by and help. Mr. Hap chopped wood whenever he came by for a visit. And Mr. Mosey would bring over a rabbit or possum. Once he even bought over half a deer! He called it venison meat and it was delicious. Auntie Lou and I had the best meal we'd had in a long time. I told Auntie it was more like "dear" meat we needed it so much. That made her sad.

I asked her how she'd made something taste so good. I wanted to learn about cooking so I could help out more. Later that night, I wrote down how she'd prepared the meat:

Auntie Lou's Venison Stew Recipe

Cut up deer meat into small cubes

Salt, pepper, flour meat

Fry in lard in cast iron pot

Cover with water and simmer 2 hours

Add cut up potatoes, carrots, onions

Cover with water and simmer 1 hour

Mix 2 tablespoons flour in 1 cup water

Add to stew, stir and cook another hour

It helped that everybody shared what they had; even if it was only beans and cornbread. Sunday was our big meal day. We'd all get together, usually at our house because it was the biggest, and the Aunt's would all cook one big meal together. If we had visitors, we'd feed them too.

The aunts decided it was time for me and Willa to learn how to cook. They let us make cornbread and biscuits and beans and rice.

Willa was supposed to fry fish one day and she battered it in flour instead of cornmeal! We all laughed at her and the boys teased she'd never get married cooking like that! But it was all we had for supper and we had to eat it; it wasn't bad.

We did have to cut back on a few things and work harder, but we were all together and I still thought that everything was all right with my world. But that year I started to feel as if I wasn't alone whenever I was outside by myself. I never saw anyone, but I had the feeling that I was being watched everywhere I went.

Auntie Lou had stopped following me so much so it wasn't her. I didn't worry none because usually I was with my cousins. Willa and I went everywhere together.

One day I went down to see if Willa could go to the well with me, but she was sick and Aunt Mozell made her stay home. Junior and Jacob were in the fields that day and Luther tagged along with me until he found out that I had to go down to the well to fetch water, then he decided he had something else to do.

I loaded two empty five gallon jugs into the wheelbarrow and set out by myself.

About half way to the well I hear whistling behind me. It sounded like Uncle Lee. Sure enough, I turn around and there he come, walking down from the mountain, from the direction of our house.

He'd been coming around some lately. First he come visit with Aunt Lila to see baby Early. One Sunday he come by when we all together having supper. Uncle Mitchell was home and Aunt Mozell's friend, Joe Peterson, was there for a visit as well so Aunt Mozell invited Uncle Lee to stay and he did. He ate a lot too!

Now here he comes around a curve in the trail whistling and jangling some coins in his overall pockets.

"Hey, Iona, how you been?" He looked me over some but not enough to make me nervous.

"Just fine, Uncle Lee, I'm gonna fetch some water," I said and walk faster.

"Well, I'ma walk on down with you," Uncle Lee said and started walking faster along with me, "help you fill up them big water jugs."

"Uh, that's OK, Uncle Lee, I can do it." I didn't think Auntie Lou was out on the trail, but if she was I didn't want her to think I'd needed his help.

"No trouble, girl. I'll just fill the jugs for you and you can git on home quicker." He whistles some more as we continue to walk down the trail.

The well was located between our house and about a mile from my Grandma Clara's old cabin. It had been six years or more since anyone had lived in the cabin, but we kept it neat.

Mr. Hap stored his handmade chairs and tables inside and Uncle Odean had also used it, to hide moonshine and homebrew. But mostly it stood empty. Every summer Auntie Lou and me made repairs to the old cabin. Aunt Lila said she might be able to rent it out again to someone in bad need.

The well lay nestled at the foot of a sloped hill surrounded by pine trees on one side and a small stream from the river on the left side. Uncle Lee stopped whistling when we got there, reached into the wheel barrow and picked up the empty water jugs. He walked down the slope and put the jugs down by the side of the well. As he unscrewed the caps, I guided the wheelbarrow down the far side which wasn't as steep. When I rolled the barrow up to the well, Uncle Lee had already started to fill the first jug with the bucket from the well.

"Whew, it's getting' warm these days," he said, lowering the empty bucket down into the cool water.

As he waited for the bucket to fill, he pulled a dirty, white handkerchief from his back pocket and wiped his round sweaty face.

"How you doin' in school?" he asked, placing the handkerchief back into the overall pocket.

"Well, some things are easy, like history, and some things are hard, like arithmetic," I say as he's filling the first jug up to the full line.

"Yeah, I know how you feel, Iona," said Uncle Lee, "but you know back when me and your uncles come along we

101

didn't get to go to school. We learn reading and writing from my daddy."

"What! For real, Uncle Lee!" I was surprised; I thought everyone had to go to school. Miz Battle said that we'd get into trouble when we didn't come to school.

"Yep, 'course our daddy also taught us a thing or two about numbers that come in handy when we had the store." For a minute he looked kinda lonely.

"Do you miss your daddy?" I asked.

He sharply looked up at me and my unease returned till he went back to filling up the water jugs.

"Nope, I'ma little too old and he been dead too long, but I do miss the store." This time when the bucket came out of the well, he took a dipper hanging from a hook at the side of the well, filled it with water and took a drink.

"You want some?" he asked and refilled the dipper with fresh, clear, cold water.

I said yes and thirstily drank as he held the dipper for me. It was so delicious I didn't even notice as some water spilled down the front of my dress.

"Well, I guess you'd better be getting on home," Uncle Lee said, loading the water jugs back onto the wheelbarrow. "Your auntie be missing you soon, I expect."

I tried to take the barrow's handles, but he wheeled it up the pathway to the top of the trail. He started to walk towards his cabin further back into the woods, but he turned around and said something which guaranteed I'd need to talk to him again.

"You know after my daddy died, my mama told me I was the head of the family." Standing in the weak, early spring sunshine, Uncle Lee seemed to look back into his distant past, perhaps thinking about his daddy.

He was a cocoa colored man with a round face and a solid round body. He had a big laugh like a jolly, fat man, but for all the roundness of body Uncle Lee was not a fat man. He narrowed his deep chocolate eyes and focused on the present.

"Do you miss your daddy, Iona?" He looked at me as I stood there with my mouth hanging open, shivering in the thin sunshine because my dress was wet with well water.

He turned and walked into the woods, still whistling that no name tune.

$*$ $*$ $*$ $*$

The year of my fourteenth birthday, I grew up and things changed forever.

I started to notice how bad off we really were. We never had money anymore, everything we had was handmade. Auntie Lou had to bargain or sell something to get something.

Uncle Lee and his woman, Essie, decided that they wanted to live in our home. They had been living in the shed Uncle Odean sometimes used to store his moonshine equipment. But now they had two children, a boy named Walker and a girl named Ruby. Uncle Lee said that they needed a bigger place because Uncle Odean might get out of prison and want his place back.

He made me and Auntie Lou move into grandma's old cabin. He said he wanted a divorce. I'd never known anyone who had been divorced. Aunt Mozell explained it as what a lot of folks did when they didn't want to be married to the other person.

Meanwhile, we'd done everything we could to survive. We sold eggs, butter, quilts, preserves and anything we could make and sell for money.

And it wasn't just me and Auntie Lou. Aunt Mozell took in washing when she didn't have a full-time job as some white lady's maid. Junior and Jacob both worked full time now in the fields. Luther worked too, but mostly during spring and summer.

Once, when we went into Somerville to shop, I overheard the white people talking about something called a depression; how rich people lost everything and committed suicide by jumping out of skyscraper buildings. I couldn't imagine what a skyscraper building looked like, but depression sure was a good name for how things felt around The Hollow.

Aunt Lila got money from Uncle Mitchell on a regular basis, but they had two children now. Willa and I finally got the girl we'd waited for so long! Her name was Pearl, like the stone in Aunt Lila's wedding ring.

Miz EJ had moved away for a while. When Uncle Odean got arrested, she'd moved to wait for the law to stop snooping around; she said it was bad for business.

At first, when she came back to The Hollow, she'd only sell to her regulars, as she called them. Men like Mr. Mosey, Mr. Hap, Uncle Lee, Uncle Mitchell when he was home, and a few others. But soon the juke joint was doing well again and anybody who had some money eventually found their way to Miz EJ. Some folks always made sure they had money for the moonshine and brew.

Aunt Lila started making homebrew and selling it to Miz EJ. I heard Aunt Mozell tell Miz Dora that at one time Aunt Lila drank a lot and she started making homebrew the way she liked it, adding things to the batches Uncle Odean made. She said that everyone always said it was the best they'd ever tasted.

One day Aunt Lila said to me that I should help her make a batch of brew; that if I learn how to make it I'll always have something to fall back on. She said 'its like sewin' and cookin',' just another way for me to survive. Sounded like more work to me but I wrote it down like I did my other recipes so I'd never forget.

Home Brew

1 quart malt

5 pounds sugar

3 yeast cakes

5 gallons water

Enough mason jars to fill large (gallon)

Glass containers

Secret ingredients

    -substitute or mix white & brown sugar

    -mix water with vanilla or other flavoring

    -add seasonal fruit at end of cycle

Aunt Lila added the malt extract into a half gallon of warm water, till it was mixed. We took turns stirring it. Next we added in the sugar, yeast cakes and the rest of the water and stirred it again. The brew had to sit for a long time, around three days.

We stored it in the old root cellar with the meats, preserves and vegetables. Auntie Lila told me the root cellar was where her parents got together for the first time.

"Course they already knew each, daddy's family use to own mama's folks when they was slaves." We were in the root cellar checking on how well the brew had settled.

"How do we know when it's ready?" I asked, interrupting the story in my excitement over becoming a master moonshiner. Junior was jealous that I got to learn how and he had to go pick cotton in the fields.

"Well, you'll know one way or 'nother," she said as she removed the rags we'd placed over each glass jar. "If it ain't ready or done right, it could explode!"

"What?" I asked and backed away from the closest jug.

Aunt Lila laughed at me and told me to notice the bubbles popping across the surface of the brown liquid. Each pop released a meaty odor into the damp root cellar.

"That's when you know you done good! Now get them pieces of cotton gauze so we can strain it into these smaller jars." Aunt Lila had gathered the jars all together at one end of the cellar.

As I covered each jar mouth with a strip of gauze, Aunt Lila ladled the brew and continued to tell me the story of how her parents fell in love. A violent storm raged outside and they got trapped in the cellar. When the storm was over, they discovered they were in love.

The homebrew took another few weeks to finish. Every three days or so you had to check it, strain it and add something else, usually the secret ingredient of whatever fruit was available. Auntie Lila wouldn't let me taste it, but she tasted it every time and sometimes she'd add more sugar to the mix.

Finally, it was ready!

Aunt told me I could take it to Miz EJ and she'd share what she made with me! I was so proud. Auntie Lou would be pleased to know that we would have some extra money.

Since we'd had to move into grandma's old house, Auntie Lou stopped talking again. She worked from early morning until you couldn't see by candlelight at night. Fall was already here and winter soon behind. I knew that Auntie Lou worked hard so we'd make it through the winter.

That morning I loaded as much as I could carry into my wheelbarrow. Willa and I were going to take turns wheeling the liquid money down to Miz EJ's house.

Everything seemed so beautiful and peaceful that afternoon. The weather was still warm, but evening had already started coming early. The birds were busy doing whatever they had to do for winter. Squirrels and rabbits collected nuts and fussed over everything that stopped them from their duties. It seemed as if the whole world was busy this late fall afternoon.

At first, I wasn't quite listening when Willa started talking. I was thinking about what we might buy with my earnings, but something she said made me immediately pay attention.

"What's that Willa?" I say, stopping dead in my tracks.

"Why, you haven't even been listening." Tears shimmered in Willa's round, black eyes.

"Willa, what's wrong?" I asked, lowering the wheel barrow down on the hard packed, dirt trail.

Willa started crying, big boohoos that turned those tear bubbles into a gusher.

For the first time in a long time I took a good look at my cousin. Lately we'd both been so busy, me and Auntie Lou working so hard for every penny. And I knew that Willa had to do all the chores around home when Aunt Mozell worked. She had three brothers to cook, clean and care for. I realized that it'd been a long time since me and my best friend had spent any time together, just the two of us talking like when we were younger.

We stood there in the middle of that country road hugging each other as if for dear life.

The tears didn't stop coming for a long while. Willa picked up the hem of her cotton shift and wiped away snot, tears and sweat. She was only four years younger, but she looked about five years old. She was thinner than I'd remembered, but so was I; we rationed our food now.

Willa usually took good care of her hair. It wasn't as fine like mine and Aunt Lila, and it always took a hard straightening. As we'd grown up, Willa's hair was always neater than mine; she took pride in its fullness and thickness. Now I could see that the kitchens were nappy, as were the edges. I could even see lint in her braids!

Even more shocking were the circles under her eyes as she stood in the warm autumn afternoon, darting her eyes between the red, dirt road and the woods, glancing both behind and in front of us.

"You making me scared, Willa!" I didn't know what to do or think. Something had happened to my cousin and it wasn't for the best.

"I got to tell somebody, Iona, you gotta listen and try to help me figure out what to do," Willa said, wringing her cotton shift between her small hands.

"Tell me, I'm listening, it can't be that bad," I say, but Willa start crying once again. "Can it?"

I waited until she got calm. Then she said, "It start a couple of years ago and now I don't know how to make him stop."

Willa tells me what happened.

"You know that we take turns bathing every Saturday night? We put the wash tub in the kitchen so it'll be close to the hot water heating on the stove. The boys all go first; me and mama change the water and go last.

One night, a couple of years ago, it's my turn to bathe. While I'm outside dumping the nasty water them boys wash up in, I think I hear something in the woods behind the house. When I stop to get a good listen, I don't hear nothing. I say to myself it's just one of them old dogs nosing about, so I just keep on emptying out the old water.

I already got my bathwater on the stove and it's hot and so I'm ready to get into the tub. You know how you gotta mix the hot water and the cold water to get it just right? Well, I do that and just forget all about the noise I thought I heard. I take off my clothes and get in the tub, real slow. You know how it is, I gotta soak and get clean fast so mama can have her turn.

I'm leaning back in the tub, just for a minute enjoying the water. I hear a noise again right behind me, at the kitchen window! You know we just got a piece of material up at that window, never needed nothing else. It dark enough in the room anyway, only one candle burning.

Anyway I turn around, sloshing some of the water out the tub and on the floor, making a real mess. Iona, I swear I see someone standing at the window looking in on me!

Well, I start yelling loud as can be! Mama and Junior run into the room asking what's wrong. I tell 'em I think I seen somebody at the window, and Junior grab his gun and run outside; Jacob and Luther run out after him. Mama gimme the towel so I can dry off and she go look out the window to see if she see anything.

Outside I can hear the boys and the hound dogs making a lot of noise. Mama tells me to get dressed. She go and get a piece of oilcloth and nail it up at the window.

The boys don't come back for a long time, they say they split up and go all the way out to Oat Sharp Road, past the old store, up past your grandma's cabin and don't see nothing. They stop in at Aunt Lila house, but she and Uncle Mitchell say they ain't heard nothing, 'cept them loud hounds.

Mama ask me if I sure I see something at the window? I'm sure but everybody looking at me as if I'm lying. So I start crying. Mama hugs me, but the boys tease me, calling me big old crybaby.

After that I start noticing that every time I'm alone in the house, if the boys be in the field and mama gone to town, it feel like somebody watching me.

Finally, he comes out in the open and I think that it's just a game that he wants me to play with him.

He starts to follow me when I go visit Miz Dora, Aunt Lila or up to see you and Auntie Lou. At first he follows me and talk; not 'bout nothing, just how I'm doing and such. At least at first he just talks, now he doing something bad!

Iona, he done started touching me. . . he reach up and kinda run his hands across my chest. He says, 'You're getting to be a big girl, everythang lookin' good.'

Every time he see me alone, he touch me somewhere, my chest, run his hands up my dress and put them inside my underwear. All the while, telling me that I look so good, that I'm a good girl, and that I'ma be a beautiful woman."

Confused and crying even harder, Willa swears me to secrecy.

"Promise you won't tell nobody I said this! But...in the beginning, I kinda like the way he made me feel....giving me all that attention. But...when he started touching me it makes me feel funny inside and I know it gotta be something bad. But why he touching me like that, Iona? Why?

"I'm scared, and I don't know how to make him stop!" Swiping at tears and snot, Willa continued to tell me what happened.

"I's out walking back from the field the other day, you know I take the boys something to eat when they don't get they lunch before they leave the house. He sees me and come up at me from behind where I couldn't see him. He say to come into the woods 'cause he got something for me. I say what? He say, 'You gotta come and see.'

I follow him off the trail, back into the woods, and he starts touching me again, all over my body. He's got me backed up against a tree, holding me with one hand against my chest. The other hand is in my underwear.

112

I say, 'You gotta stop, please!' He say, 'Don't you want what I got for you?' I'm crying, 'Please, please stop!' He start pulling my pants off and he say, 'this gonna make you a woman.'"

ODEAN'S STORY

"You boys, slow the car down, I want to make it home in one piece!" Odean held on to his old, felt field hat with one hand, and held on to the car door for dear life with the other hand.

When Jacob and Luther picked Odean up outside the Decatur jail, it had been 11 years since they'd seen each other. At first, they didn't recognize him and he didn't recognize them.

The little nappy headed wild boys Odean remembered had grown into young men. Luther, the youngest, had a mustache and outweighed Odean by thirty pounds. Jacob was smaller, wiry like Odean had once been, and was still the wild one of all three brothers.

"Aw, Uncle, we ain't going but thirty miles an hour!" Jacob was in the driver's seat of an old battered Ford. He turned around to give Odean a dazzling smile. He looked so much like his father, Odean thought and couldn't help but sigh with sadness, missing his baby brother once again after all these years.

It was the summer of 1935.

The State of Alabama correctional facilities at Decatur released Odean Ghee after he'd served his sentence. Of course, the release may also have come after years of hard labor on the chain gang ruined his health; the state could have felt it was too expensive to feed and shelter him without the benefits of manual labor.

A persistent cough troubled Odean and he no longer stood head and shoulders above the average man. Always thin, he now appeared frail as well. Anyone seeing him for the first time would assume he was an old man of 70, when he was still a few years younger.

As the men drove the twenty miles from Decatur back to Vermosa, the young men took turns talking, filling Odean in on the lost years. As they passed through the countryside, he saw that the years had also left a mark on his homeland. The land was more beautiful than ever but most of it had been left to grow wild. The Hollow trail now barely came all the way down to Oat Sharp Road. Bramble, trees and kudzu fought for space in what had once been cleared farmland.

Parts of the old trail were impassible. It was now just about impossible to walk clear across the mountain to the other side. Many of the paths were either overgrown with eager kudzu or rutted out by harsh weather conditions.

Odean's old shack was hardly visible through the flowers, vines and shrubbery that had grown over the structure. It had been a long time since Lee and his second family lived in the old place. Always well hidden, the woods had taken it back.

A mini junkyard sprouted in one pasture that had always been prized for the best fiddle worms in the county. Jacob and Luther had discovered a fascination for cars and purchased spare parts whenever they could afford it. The pasture now served as a place they examined engines, pulled them apart and tried putting them back together. Their pride and joy, a 1926 Model T built from the ground up, was sheltered under a lean-to shack. One day, they told Odean, they would make it run as fast as a streak of lighting!

Odean understood that not only had The Hollow changed, but that the South had changed as well. Still the home of good ole boys, cotton crops and the KKK; change was well underway everywhere, moving like kudzu over that which didn't get out of the way of progress.

The younger generation, Negroes and whites, had become restless. Many moved away forever. Negroes poured out of the South as fast as they could afford a one-way train ticket. Well-off whites sent sons and daughters away to school; many never returned home.

America had a brief fling with prosperity, followed by the awful thing called a depression that moved south, bringing with it mill closures and layoffs, low prices for cotton crops and high prices for everything else. As usual, Negroes suffered the most. And now, there were whispers that another war might be brewing.

Odean listened as the boys filled him in on how the Ghees suffered along with everyone else. Their one saving grace was in the ability to make the best moonshine in three counties. Lila and Iona continued to supply EJ, while adding on new customers, including Junior, who after all these years fulfilled his wishes to become a 'shiner.

Odean chuckled at the memory of teaching Lila how to make homebrew. He remembered thinking it would take her mind off losing baby Truly. Now it seemed she had turned it into a moneymaker better than his own had been.

Luther and Jacob talked of one day moving north, perhaps to Michigan where automobiles were built in huge factories. Luther was close to his dream; he told Odean that he was on his way north before year's end.

He wanted to own a service station or maybe even an automobile repair shop.

Junior had a honky-tonk in Madison County. He said it was because it was closer to Huntsville, considered the big city, and closer to more folks who could afford the going rate for a jug. Jacob laughed that it was also the home of Billie Watkins, a Southern flower Junior was sweet on and now lived with.

Jacob and Luther were sweet on automobiles and they worked for Gus Petty who owned a combination service station and garage. They also ran errands for Lila and worked weekends with Junior. These afterhour duties afforded them extra money they needed to buy the beloved spare parts and to keep them in the latest model Fords they loved.

Odean saw that Jacob turned out to be just as wild as his daddy had been, wooing women wherever he went. In the streets of Decatur he'd made it a point of speaking to every good looking gal who crossed paths with them. He was handsome, tall, and had a natural talent for music. Hat

Man, the local blues singer, taught him how to play guitar. Luther said Jacob often accompanied his playing with a voice that was "not too bad." Jacob promised to serenade him later that evening.

Luther appeared serious and cautious. Odean would soon find out that everyone turned to him for his suggestions and advice. Everyone said he was smart enough to go to college; and he dreamed of attending Alabama A&M in Huntsville. He was already 16 and didn't have much schooling, having worked in the fields most of his youth, but Mozell secretly put money aside anyway just in case those dreams were realized.

Odean was shocked to find out that Willa had already moved up north. Barely 14 when she'd run away with a blues player, Willa soon found herself pregnant and broke. She eventually found factory work and settled in Pontiac, Michigan.

Luther said Willa would put them up and help get them jobs in the automobile plant whenever they were ready. He was ready now, but Jacob was the one who couldn't pull himself away from the sporting life as a moonshine runner and blues player.

Lila and Mitchell had two additional rooms built onto their house and seemed to be doing well. Mitchell still worked as a porter for the L&N Railroad, however, the older he got the less work he seemed to get; younger men were more in demand. He was home more often now and Lila was pleased.

Odean learned that since he had been gone a few new family members had been welcomed. Children were always a happy constant in a changing world. Early and Pearl belonged to Lila and Mitchell. Both had started school and Pearl was not far behind Early in grade but definitely ahead in smarts.

Lee also had a boy and girl, Ruby and Walker. Odean was surprised to learn that Lee had divorced Lou and put her and Iona out of the family home and that they had lived in Clara's old cabin for a while.

Mason was the newest addition and belonged to Iona; she had moved to Huntsville several years ago and found work in the Sunny Farm Bakery plant. She was content for the time being but they thought she was planning to move again before too long.

The boys told him their mama, Mozell, finally married Joe Peterson. He'd hung around long enough, they seemed to imply. Odean remembered Joe and thought that he was a good man.

With all her children grown and on their own, Mozell didn't have to work as much although she still took in washing and ironing whenever she could. For the most part, she usually watched the children while the younger women worked.

But, life and death go hand in hand. This time, Odean was shocked to learn, it had claimed the lives of Mosey, Lou and Essie. Essie had been Lee's woman and mother of Walker and Ruby.

Jacob and Luther had no problem explaining how Mosey died. He went peaceful. He'd developed a bad cold one winter, after falling asleep on his back porch. Drunk, folks said. The cold turned into pneumonia and before the home remedies could work, he was gone.

Soon after the funeral, Dora moved to Huntsville to live with their daughter Betty.

The Thomas house didn't stay vacant long. Odean's old friend Hap moved in, allowing him to be closer to his Cousin Mitchell's family, and closer to EJ. He settled in, sharecropping to pay his rent.

At the end of it all, Odean still had many questions. Among them, what happened to Lou and Lee's other woman, Essie? How was Iona doing without Lou?

Luther and Jacob didn't have the answers. Odean got the feeling that there were some things they didn't want to talk about, mostly the deaths of Lou and Essie. They did tell him EJ was well and offered to drop him off at her place first.

"Miz EJ will tell you 'bout Auntie Lou and Miz Essie, Uncle," said Jacob as he swung the Ford onto the rutted trail leading up to the juke joint.

"Uncle Lee say they kill each other," Luther said and looked at Jacob, perhaps seeking approval or confirmation. "Uncle Lee found the bodies."

"Odean, it's good to see you after all these years!" EJ flung her arms around Odean's frail shoulders, all but crushing him in her excitement. She couldn't help but notice how ill he looked.

"EJ, you shore looking good," Odean bent to kiss her check, but she turned her head just in time for the old friend's lips to brush together. Odean blinked, but didn't pull away.

She hoped she did look good. When the boys let her know they'd drop him off at her place first thing, she washed and ironed her best dress, a lemon yellow, flower print affair; she'd fixed her hair and asked Iona to come by and help her make up her face. She felt silly all gussied up but she wanted the first meeting, after all this time, to be one where he'd realize that she'd been waiting for him to come home, home to her.

They looked at each other with true fondness and hugged again just because it felt good.

"Where the boys go?" EJ asked.

"Oh, they said they'd come after me in a few hours," Odean answered. "You know I barely made it up that trail. I had to sit a spell under them Walnut trees. Use to be a time . . ."

EJ noticed once again how worn out Odean looked.

"Don't you worry none about that, what you want to drink? You ought to have a taste of Lila's shine; you won't believe how good it is. You did good teaching that one. Did the boys tell you that she also make the best wine in the entire county? Blueberry, Muscadine, Lord, she even got the church women buying!" EJ talked on, nervous for the first time since Odean walked through her front door.

"I think I'ma have to wait a spell on the drinking. Water be just fine," Odean found a seat and looked around the

121

large room that was a recent add on. "I see you finally got some privacy from the juke joint. This looks good."

"Yea. Mosey, Mitchell and the boys built this for me 'bout three years ago." EJ went to a small washstand and poured water from a jug into a clean glass. "You know I'd left The Hollow for a spell?"

"I heard. I didn't get visitors often. Lee come visit often the first few years and Mitchell stopped by a few years ago when the train stopped in Decatur."

"Well, you know I had to keep away from them revenuers. I could a paid them off, but I figured laying low and let them think they had run me out of business was the best thing, hell the only thing, to do."

"That's God's truth. I wish I had seen 'em coming, I would a lain low too!" They both laughed and EJ joined Odean, handing him the glass of water before sitting in one of her cane chairs.

He drank nearly all the water before putting down the glass. It was fresh well water just like he remembered it – delicious.

"EJ, the boys filled me in on just about everythang that done happened these past years, just one thang they said you'd be the best to tell me. How did Lou and this woman Essie die?"

EJ stood up and went over to the screen door, looking out toward the trail. Lately she'd begun to imagine that every time certain things were mentioned, even the woods seemed to listen. As if waiting to approve or disapprove of the conversation.

She'd known this moment would come. It was only natural that he'd have questions. She'd practiced what to say. But now that she had to put truth to the lie, she found herself unable to look at him as she talked. So, she started by telling him what was already known. She figured if he still had questions after hearing the story, Lila might be the best person to tell him what they all feared.

"It been about four or so years ago now. I remember it was fall. I'd been back about a year. Folks had started coming by again. You know, just the regulars. Hell, Mosey use to keep me with spending money! He say, he so glad I come home he'd do anything to keep me in this place........I surely do miss him.

"Well, Lila done started selling some shine on the side. Early had just been born and she had a few more expenses. Oh, by the way, did you know she taught Iona a few of her secrets? Oh, don't worry; Lila thought she was too young back then to make the hard stuff, so she starts her off on the homebrew. She do a good job of it too.

"I was waiting for the 'brew that day. Iona usually brung it in the late evening before folks come in from the fields. I remember thinking, she taking a long time, but I gets busy. A few men from the mill showed up but that was alright, 'cause they got money for shine. The brew mostly for folks going through tough times and don't have much money to waste.

"One girl I knew from when I moved away comes by with a wagon load of folks straight from the fields. It be about six of them, including my friend Patsy, her friend Sarah, and some men I didn't know. Patsy drinks homebrew so I tell her that I'm low. But they stay a spell, the women drink my 'brew till it's gone. By the time they leave, it already late.

"It didn't look like nobody else coming. Mosey already stopped in for a taste and gone on home to Dora. I's cleaning up when I hear a noise behind me. When I turn around I see Lee. He's standing just inside the door covered with blood; blood all over him, on his shoes, overalls and shirt sleeves and hands."

EJ finally turned away from the screen door. She looked at Odean and thought about how she had felt when she turned around and seen Lee standing there. He looked like a man in a world of trouble, like a Negro caught in a KKK round up.

She noticed that Odean didn't look too good either. She picked up the water glass, went back to the washstand and opened the door and reached inside for the bottle of liquor she kept for emergencies.

EJ filled the glass the same as she had for the water, all the way to the top. Odean didn't comment when she gave him the full glass. At first he just looked at it with indifference, as if he'd had a shot just like it every day these last hard years. Finally he brought it to his lips, tilted his head back and drained it of every drop; he kept his eyes closed and his body shook.

Watching him take that first drink, seeing the faint color creeping into his thin checks, EJ made up her mind how her story would end.

"When I turn around he say, 'You gotta help me EJ, all hell done broke loose.'" She walked back to the screen door. Off in the distance, shadows on the mountain seemed to dart in and out of the pine, walnut and elm trees.

"Well, I could see that it had so I asked what happened. He say, 'I was in the outhouse and heard screaming.'" By the time he gets to the house, Lou and Essie in the parlor on the floor, hacking at each other with a butcher knife. The children in they room crying.

"He say he didn't know what to do, he run over and separate them. Lou already hurt real bad, he thought her throat been cut. So, he turns some attention on Essie. She hurt bad too, been stabbed in the chest.

'Fore too long, Essie die in his arms. When he can, he say he check on Lou again but she dead too.

"Lee say everything happen so fast he don't know exactly how it all got started. He say he think Lou turned up at the house with the butcher knife and attacked Essie. Maybe she still mad 'cause he put her and Iona out of the house so he can move in Essie and the children. They get to fighting and Essie somehow gets the knife and defends herself, killing Lou."

Feeling Odean's eyes on her back, EJ turned away from the darting shadows on the mountainside. The hard part was over, she knew she could now sit with him and continue talking about that awful night.

"The children were crying, and Walker, that's Lee's oldest, had got out of bed and come into the room calling for his mama. Lee say he knew he had to get them away from that awful scene, so he saddled up and take them down to Mozell and tell her what done happen. He come by and tell me on his way to the sheriff – no use going to get Doc Baker he say 'cause they already dead.

"You know we got a new sheriff now? Sheriff Moores finally got what he deserved; went to one of those white juke joints and got shot dead.

"After Lee left, I go up to see what I could do to help. When I get there Lila was standing in the shotgun hallway crying. She tell me Mozell sent Junior to let her know and she come straight away hoping it wasn't true.

"Between the two of us, we clean the room and wash the bodies. It was the hardest thing I ever had to do in my life, never want to see anything like it ever again.

"By the time Lee got back with the sheriff, we had cleaned up everything and I was plumb worn out. It just tore me up inside having to bathe Lou. That poor woman never had a good day in her life and now she gone."

They sat together for a while, just two old friends sharing family news. After a while, EJ noticed that the forest sounds had returned. The wind blew through the trees, birds sang, bees hummed and other small creatures talked among themselves in the trees and undergrowth.

She guessed that, for a while, everything was alright.

JACOB'S SONG

Junior always gave his Saturday nights a theme; tonight was "Blues, Nothing but the Blues." Jacob was performing.

It had been more than a year since Luther moved to Detroit. Jacob decided to stay in the South so that he could gain more experience playing in small bands.

He got together a small group that played on Saturday nights twice a month at the honky-tonk: Six Fingers on Jew harp and harmonica, and Buster Man on horn. Jacob sang and played guitar.

Business was good. They played for tips, folks put change in the copper kettle Jacob kept by his chair. He knew who paid and who didn't, and he made sure folks who paid had a good time.

Jacob had a few new songs he'd written and strung together. He did the old favorites, took special requests from his regulars and included the newest tunes from the big boys, but he always threw in some of his own. So, far they'd been well received.

At the end of the first set, he had his eye on the new gal helping his brother out behind the makeshift bar and he was ready to make his move.

"Folks, you all know I likes to try out a new song every now and then. Give a listen to this one. I call it 'Blues Come Knocking.' Let me know if you like it, and if you don't like it, don't let me know." He laughed along with the crowd and strummed the guitar before nodding to the band to join in. Throwing his head back he moaned.

> Blues knock on my front door
>
> I say nobody here,
>
> Blues knock on my front door I yell out, you can't come in
>
> I hear you knocking
>
> I hear you tapping
>
> Rapping on my front door
>
> But you ain't gonna get in
>
> Blues knock on my back door
>
> I say nobody here
>
> Blues knock on my back door I yell you can't come in
>
> I'm closed up for the night
>
> Closed up real tight
>
> I'm home for the night
>
> You can't get in
>
> Blues knocking on my door
>
> I'm ready to fight
>
> Blues knocking on my door
>
> But he can't get in tonight
>
> Oh, lawd you won't get in tonight

They loved it. The men stood and yelled, clapping work callused hands together so loud it sounded like thunder.

The women, some dainty some loud, called out special kinds of encouragement. Jacob drunk it all in; this was what he lived for and why he hadn't followed his baby brother Luther up north. When he became more successful he planned to tour the northern cities, including Detroit where Luther and Willa lived.

The band took a break. Jacob was slapped on the back so many times he started to feel bruised. He forgot the pain as soon as the woman smiled at him from behind the six-foot long piece of wood planking set on water barrels Junior called his bar.

"What you want, sugar," asked the prettiest woman he'd seen tonight. She had a smoky voice to match the smoky room. Chocolate skin looked good enough to eat. Her hair was all pulled back in a school teacher bun, but those red lips said kiss me, daddy!

"I'll take anything you got, baby, if you keep on talking like that," Jacob said. He could tell they was gonna get along real well. He watched her walk away and couldn't help but notice that she had everything he liked and in all the right places.

She glanced over her shoulder once to make sure he was watching, then switched down the narrow aisle between the bar and wooden crates stacked up to waist level. Grabbing a glass from the built-in shelves under the bar top, she bent over, making sure she gave him a good view of her best side.

Jacob leaned over to get a better look. He licked his lips in anticipation when another slap on the back just about shoved him over the bar.

"Down, hound dog, down, boy!" Junior grinned from ear to ear seeing the startled expression on his brother's face change to one of pleasure.

The brothers stood and embraced. They had reason to celebrate. Junior was a new daddy! His girlfriend, Billie, delivered a big whopper of a baby girl two days ago. Jacob hadn't had time to visit yet, but tonight he'd sure have time to celebrate with his big brother.

"You the one you ole bull! How many this one make?" Jacob teased. Junior had the real thing with Billie. In fact, he was surprised that they weren't married yet.

Junior blushed, about to make a quick comeback when the chocolate beauty placed a glass in front of the men.

"Oh, Jacob, got somebody I know you wanna meet. This is a friend of Billie, name's Dorothy but call her Dot. This my brother, Jacob, Dot; give him whatever he needs."

"I'ma sure do my best. Pleased to meet you, Jacob. Let me know if you want anything else," Dot leaned forward with her smoky words, giving Jacob an excellent view down her low-cut, close fitting black dress before walking away to serve another thirsty customer.

"Boy, put them eyes back in your skull," laughed Junior as he led his brother toward a table and chairs he kept reserved for his special guests.

Jacob couldn't resist giving Dot another glance. He was pleased to see that she did not give the new customer – a big, black, heavy man – the same treatment she'd given him.

He walked behind his brother noticing that Junior had picked up a few pounds. Never as tall as his little brothers, Junior took after his mama's side of the family. They had round bodies and round faces. On the women it looked good. Junior had the Ghee cheekbones and high slanted eyes. They saved him from being ordinary.

The brothers settled into their chairs and talked for a while about the baby and Junior's favorite topic of conversation, Billie. Secretly, Jacob thought it wasn't good to love a woman like his brother seemed to love Billie, but he sensed Junior needed to talk so he listened while glancing around the room.

They had a good crowd tonight, crowded but not enough so you couldn't find a seat. The place also had a good mix of women and men. That was good, because generally if there weren't enough women to go around the men would usually get to fighting by the end of the evening. Enough women in the place and a man's chances were better of not going home alone.

Junior had a fine place, one of the best around in three counties. After three years it was well established. Known as Junior's Joint, it set well back on a winding road that often came close to the river; there were a few dirt roads that led inland. Junior's Joint was off one of these roads next to the muddy river.

Junior's reason for success was twofold. One, he paid off the local sheriff, but he made sure that his reported earnings were way less than what he actually made. Two, he had a backup man. Big Top Tom was a giant of a man who loved nothing better than busting drunken heads together. Big Top kept order one way or, as he liked to say, his way.

The joint was fairly large. The one room held seven or eight tables that could comfortably hold four people each; six more could stand up at the make shift bar. Add a few more standing round in the corners and gathered round outside and on a good night like tonight the joint would serve 30 or more folks.

In a separate back room on Friday and Saturday nights you could order fried fish or chicken sandwiches.

Everybody enjoyed the music, dancing, drinking and visiting with friends. Big Top sat on a backless chair over by the front door, checking out the activities. From time to time he'd smile to himself, as if to say 'alright, now that's the way to act and if ya'll don't continue to act like that I'ma bust some heads.'

Jacob saw Six Fingers at a table with three admiring women. The short, little man wasn't much to look at, but he was a flashy dresser. Tonight the audience had been treated to black and white Stacy Adams, and a dark maroon, colored suit with a green tie.

Six Fingers did have a sixth finger; it was on his right hand. The finger was small and stunted, but on it he wore a baby size, gold ring. He was the more experienced of the trio; he'd played in Birmingham, Atlanta and even Nashville. Jacob planned to go on the road with him next time he decided to head out on a tour.

Buster Man sat on a chair behind Big Top with his back to the room, stroking his horn. He was the quiet one and the first one back on stage when it was time to play; he didn't care about nothing but his horn. Buster was average, about Jacob's size; he kept his head shaved and always wore a hat. Tonight's choice was straw with a rolled up brim.

Jacob tuned back in time to hear Junior say he'd gotten a letter from Luther.

"He say things going real well. He's still saving up to move into his own place but he got a car, a Ford, of course. No woman yet, but then Luther never was a stud like you." They both laughed at this image.

"Yea, well, I done selected my heifer for the evening. Tell me something about Dot, she got a man?" Jacob picked up his drink and leaned back in his chair, noticing that Buster was headed back, signaling it was time to play again.

"Can't say, I only met her day 'fore yesterday. Billie mama sent for her to come help out for awhile," Junior seemed thoughtful for a minute, "I don't rightly know if it gonna be a good idea or not."

"Why you say that, man, she'll be good for the place. Look how many men flocked up 'round that bar." They both turned to look. It was true. Dot did a brisk business. Men crowded together at the bar and watched her every move.

Some she joked with, some she didn't give more than a few words.

"Well, I hear tell she use to work in the city at the Sweet Shack. Some men got to fighting over her. One got shot. I don't think he died or nothing, but you know I can't have that kind of thing going on 'round here. Sheriff put me out of business, least for a while."

"Oh, man, you know that fat ass sheriff ain't gonna let nothing mess with his extra money. Besides you got Big Top. Anything starts up and they'll be out 'fore they can say mama!"

The brothers laughed at the idea. They both knew that it was true. Big Top had a sharp eye. He often broke up a fight before those involved even knew they were going to fight.

The only time they'd ever seen Big Top flustered was one night when two women, Janie and Peggy, got into it over who had on the prettiest dress. When Big Top recovered from seeing women rolling around on the dirt floor, he lifted them one under each arm, took them out back and threw them into the river! After that, there'd been no more cat fights at Junior's Joint.

Jacob promised Junior he'd come see the newest addition to the Ghee family soon and got up to join the band for another set.

All night long Jacob kept his eye on Dot. He could tell that she kept her eye on him as well. When women he knew came up to request a tune or to ask him something more personal, he noticed that she paid extra attention until the women went back to their tables. It gave him a happy feeling all the way down to his Johnson!

So he sang the blues with a smile. From time to time he stopped his horny thoughts long enough to check out the crowd, to make sure they were having a good time, to thank those who stopped by to add a donation to the copper pot.

Jacob noticed Junior sit at a table filled with his closest friends, John Thomas, Nat Locke and Seth Rogers. The men seemed to be having a good time, laughing, congratulating Junior on the baby.

That's when he noticed a man who appeared to be a stranger sitting alone behind his brother and his friends. The man did not appear to be having a good time. He scowled over his drink and threw dark glances at his brother's table and in the direction of the bar.

Jacob saw Big Top leave the front door and walk over to the wall, to the left of the bar, behind the scowling man's table. There he stood like a giant, silent tree with his arms across his chest. Everything seemed to be under control.

It was late, just about closing time. Jacob turned to Six Fingers and Buster Man; they discussed playing two, maybe three more tunes, ending with "Blues Come Knocking."

They were into the second tune, a local favorite by Country Boy Slim. It was mostly a non-vocal arrangement and Jacob's head was hung down, not thrown back in his singing style. That's why he missed the commotion when it started.

He looked up in time to see Big Top grab the scowling man he'd noticed earlier by the neck and the seat of the pants, lifting him off his feet. He threw the man against the closest wall. A few women screamed but the male customers suggested Big Top do drastic things to the drunken man's body.

Jacob knew the only thing to do was to keep playing until everything was taken care of. As the trio played on, he watched as Big Top held the man while Junior searched him for a knife, gun or anything that might cause harm. Finding nothing, they escorted him outside the club. Big Top took an occasional opportunity to smack the poor man upside his head.

Jacob played on but stayed alert for trouble; only relaxing when he saw his brother walk back into the room followed by Big Top. You never knew how things would turn out; it was a good policy to be alert.

Happy feelings returned as Jacob went back to thinking of just what he and Dot would do when he offered her a ride home after closing. They'd come to the last song. His song.

> Blues knocking on my door
>
> I'm ready to fight
>
> Blues knocking on my door
>
> But he can't get in tonight
>
> Oh, lawd you won't get in tonight

It still felt good to hear them clapping for him. He already had plans for another little ditty. It just might be ready the next time he and the band got together.

As was the custom, soon as they finished, Junior come up and thanked everybody for coming and helping him pay his bills. He told them to take care and come again, but Junior's Joint was closed for the night; you don't have to go home but you gotta get the hell out.

Six Fingers and Jacob got up and exchanged a few words with friends. Buster Man stayed on the stage, rag in hand already polishing his horn. Six Fingers made arrangements with one of the women he'd sat with earlier, leading her to a table so she could wait for him.

The room took some time to empty, most folks being too drunk to hurry. Only the regulars kept their seats; Junior's friends, one or two women who sat on their laps, and Big Top who was always the last to leave. Dot rinsed glasses behind the bar.

Jacob gathered up the copper pot and started counting the coins. It was always split between the three of them. Didn't matter that he was the lead singer; without the experience of Six Fingers and the dependability of Buster Man, he'd still be strumming his guitar out in the field.

Junior came over while he counted out the money and Jacob asked about the trouble. The man was Dot's old friend. Someone she'd given the heave-ho to before coming out to work for Junior. He'd found out where she was and figured she'd have another man before too long. He implied that Junior was that man.

His name was Reece Jones. When the liquor gave him enough courage, he'd walked over to the bar and grabbed Dot, but before he could do anything Big Top was on him. When they walked him outside, Big Top explained why it wasn't a good idea for him to come back. The last they seen, he'd been in his car headed up the river road.

Jacob volunteered to take Dot home; Junior thought that would be ok, but warned him to be careful.

The trio made a tidy sum that night. They got mostly quarters, usually it was nickels and dimes, but a few flush folks had even put in folding green. Even Six Fingers was pleased. He said that Jacob's singing and writing had improved so much they should think about trying it out on the road, maybe in Birmingham.

Jacob was excited as he escorted Dot to his automobile. Those happy feelings were back in full force as Dot pressed against his side, rubbing against him like a well-fed cat. He ran one hand down over her ample backside, squeezing it. She made a soft moan.

He couldn't wait; he needed to kiss those lips, to run his tongue down between that chocolate valley that peeped out at him from her dress top. Jacob leaned his guitar case up against the fender and sat the Mason jar containing his money down beside it. He pulled Dot into his arms.

Wasn't nothing like having a warm, willing woman in your arms.

Before he could kiss those delicious red lips something cold slide around his throat and pulled him out of Dot's embrace. He wanted to visit that deep, chocolate valley but instead he lay sprawled on his back staring at the stars and a half moon. Dot's moan now sounded like a scream.

RUBY'S STORY

Ruby took her time walking up the trail. Sunlight flashed between the tree leaves, tracing a tic-tack-toe path across her unhappy face. Alabama was in the middle of a drought, and everything was dry yet heavy with southern humidity.

The noonday silence meant that the forest creatures were wise and slumbered away the hottest part of the day.

Ruby wished she could sleep through the unbearable heat. She hated the weather; lately she hated just about everything. She tugged at the homemade white shorts that stuck to her sweaty legs and tightened her grip on the galvanized bucket she carried in her right hand and continued walking downhill to the fresh water well nestled at the foot of a sloped hill surrounded by pine trees.

Ruby flopped down beneath the fragrant trees, among the pine needles, and looked out over the land. The heavy silence should have eased her troubled mind, and the smell of pine cones should have made her think of Johnson's Hole, her favorite fishing place. Instead, with a deep sigh that moved up from her dusty bare feet, and a toss of her reddish braids, all she could think about was her Uncle Odean.

He'd been home for over two years and seemed to always be sick. Something was wrong in his chest. He coughed a lot.

Ruby's favorite uncle, her father and most of the other men she knew lived a hard life of homemade liquor, heavy field work, and in Odean's case, heavy smoking.

A sudden rustling in the grass startled her, but it was only a grasshopper.

She climbed out of her miserable daydream and filled the bucket from the deep well. Her copper toned skin glistened with sweat and the red braids framed a scowling face. Ruby finally started out for home.

She didn't want to be late fixing supper. Tonight it would be red beans with ham hocks, rice, cabbage and cornbread. In spite of her earlier unhappiness, she hummed as she cooked. Uncle Odean would be over for supper and she wanted it to be special.

They had a rather large family; everyone usually gathered at Aunt Lila's or Aunt Mozell's house, laughing, talking, and sharing with family members or friends who dropped by for a visit.

The screen door open and closed so quietly that Ruby knew her Aunt was home from work. If the screen door slammed, it meant either her brother Walker or Cousin Early was home. Everyone else usually called out a greeting.

Uncle Mitchell wasn't home; work would keep him away for another month or so. Cousin Pearl had gone into the city to visit with Iona and would not be back. Everyone else was expected to come for dinner.

Ruby called out a word of greeting and walked through the house towards her Aunt's bedroom. She stood in the doorway, stirring the contents of a bowl she held in her hands and watched Lila sit down in an old wooden rocker.

Lila looked up at Ruby with a smile and noticed the limp braids and the shine of perspiration across the girl's frowning face. Lila had thought Ruby a dedicated tomboy who would never buckle under to kitchen chores, housekeeping or dresses. Now, bowl in hand, she looked nearly domestic.

"What's the matter, baby, you hot?" Lila lifted her skirts and fanned her face.

"It sure is hot, but supper's just about ready. I just have to put this crackling bread in the oven." Ruby had just learned how to make crackling bread; it was her uncle's favorite. "You want me to make some lemonade?"

A reply came from the front hallway before Lila could respond.

"Well, if Lila don't want lemonade, I sure do. How long y'all gonna keep a man thirsty?" Odean called from the kitchen.

Ruby hurried to meet him, still holding the bowl in one hand. She prattled on about her delicious crackling bread, the best he'd ever had, and she'd fix some lemonade right away, and Aunt Lila would be out soon as she changed her clothes.

Even as she chattered away she could not but note how thin he was. Seemed even thinner than when she'd seen

143

him just last week; the honey brown skin stretched across his sharp cheekbones. Odean settled into one of the kitchen chairs. Ruby watched him so he gave her a quick smile, dimples flashing.

"I'll make a big pitcher of lemonade just as soon as I get this bread into the oven," Ruby said, pouring the thick mixture, lumpy with pieces of fried crackling, into a hot iron skillet.

Noticing that neither of his nephews was at home Odean asked after them.

"Walker and Early off somewhere together. I imagine them in town hooting after fast women." Ruby put the skillet into the oven and stepped back from the heat.

"Now, don't go on, they young men now. Young men, sometimes old ones too, need to be around pretty women." Odean chuckled at the expression on Ruby's face. It seemed to say, 'well we don't need them.'

Odean continued, "It gonna be a long time before he get another chance to court if the Army got anything to say about it." They all were concerned about Early. He'd gotten his call from Uncle Sam and was scheduled to report within the year.

"What's this about courting?" Lila asked as she stepped into the room. She'd changed into a simple homemade blouse and skirt which did not take away from her beauty; she was still tall and trim. Only her salt and pepper hair betrayed her age. "Baby, you thinkin' on courtin'?"

"Naw! I don't even like boys!" Ruby was indignant at the thought. "They are stupid and nasty." This wasn't quite true. She'd noticed a couple of boys, but so far none who she wanted to court.

"That's good baby, don't get started too young, you never know..." Behind them the floor boards in the hallway squeaked, and Lila's reply was left unspoken.

They all looked up as Lee came into the room. He stood in the doorway for a moment, looked first at his brother, said hi to Ruby before giving Lila a brief glance. His smile of greeting was for Odean.

Lila barely greeted her brother before helping Ruby soften the lemons by rolling them against a board. They sliced the lemons and squeezed them into a glass pitcher. Cool well water was added; Ruby added sugar enthusiastically until Lila stopped her from using the entire sack.

The men carried on a conversation, mostly about Early and Walker, but some about other family members.

Lee was pleased he'd listened to Luther a few years back. The young man had suggested he stop planting so much cotton and focus instead on planting peanuts and corn. Now peanuts, corn and money received from renting pasture land out to Mr. Pitney, kept them going. Cotton farming was for the big farmers now; heavy machinery had replaced field labor.

Lee asked after EJ, Odean allowed how she was alright but since folks were able to get around better these days, business wasn't good. In fact, she had considered closing down again. She was a good cook; she could sell pies, cakes and pastries to the white stores in Teluchi, Somerville and Decatur.

They heard Walker and Early outside before they even opened the door. The two young men burst into the room still joking with each other. Soon the conversation was all about the young men, where they had been and what they were doing.

Supper was soon ready. Lila and Ruby joined the men, and the conversation turned to the upcoming family reunion. It had been a long time since the family had gotten together. Early's draft and Odean's return was just what they needed to put on a good shindig.

Ruby was excited, and did most of the talking, which was usual. Walker and Early ate up everything in sight and told Ruby that her cooking had gotten better. Lila was quiet. Odean was also a quiet person, and coughing spells made talking difficult for him.

As was his habit, Lee watched them each in turn. Occasionally laughing his beer belly laugh at something the young men said.

*   *   *   *

Oh Mary don't you weep
don't weep, tell Martha not

146

to moan, tell Martha not to
mooaan!

It was so hot in Second Baptist that the whole choir sang in D flat. No lively solos either.

Mother Rice, piano player and choir leader, couldn't fan while playing the piano so she hurriedly ended the song by banging shut the piano lid. She was heard to mutter under her breath, "By the time services are over I'll be melted."

Pastor Crutcher frequently mopped his bald head with an already soaked handkerchief. Deacon Simms drank five glasses of water. The church sisters and mothers fanned nonstop and all the children fussed and fidgeted.

Pastor finally dismissed his damp congregation. The children ran outside while the rest of the church, wet and wilted, followed thankfully.

Ruby felt sure that the miserable weather would spoil the family reunion. She was barely civil when one of the church members approached Lila as they stood together outside under a large elm tree. Sister Mabel Dean gave her a sharp glance as Ruby sulked away from the older women to go stand beside Pearl.

"Lila, you need any help getting ready for the reunion?" Mabel inquired, fanning herself with a stiff piece of cardboard that had a photo of Anderson's Mortuary on one side. She wore a thin, gauzy dress over a white cotton slip. Ruby thought it would have been pretty if it hadn't been limp with sweat.

147

"No, I don't think so. Me and Mozell got everythang we need and Iona helpin' out as well. Willa, or Luther, should be the first to arrive; should be here by Thursday." Lila was tired and just wanted to get home.

Ruby kept her distance from the women and watched as groups of families exchanged greetings, rounded up stray children and prepared to head home for a good old fashioned Sunday supper. She saw her aunt talking to one of her cousins and Pearl waved to let her know where they were.

Uncle Mitchell was the church's treasurer and he often stayed late to count the meager offering. They would be among the last to leave.

She noticed a group of young men heading for the woods. She knew where they were going and wondered if she had enough time to sneak away and join them for a cigarette. She didn't bother asking Pearl to join her. Her cousin chatted with the Anderson twins and Ruby knew she would not want to get in trouble; she was such a goody-two-shoes.

Ruby made it to the corner of the church as Pastor and her uncle stepped outside into the heat.

"It's slim today, Pastor," Mitchell said, sticking his hands in the pockets of his shiny black trousers and leaning back on his heels. "Guess folks just too hot to give."

"Yes, Brother Black, I reckon so. Don't you worry none about it, things usually pick up." Pastor Crutcher's bald head glistened with sweat. "Don't forget to tell your folks coming home for the reunion to be sure and stop by the church next Sunday."

Mitchell smiled at Ruby as the men continued to speak about church business. It was too late to sneak away so she walked back to where Lila and Pearl waited by the car. It wasn't too long before the rest of the family joined them and they settled down for the hot ride home.

Second Baptist soon disappeared behind them and a graveled road carried them homeward. The hot weather had not diminished the countryside's beauty. Here and there a country store, decorated with tin advertisements, offered sodas, poultry feed and other staples for sale.

The gravel road led off onto a road of red dirt which rose up behind the car and covered everything before settling down again.

Summer seemed never ending. The relentless heat woke you up in the morning and settled in with you at bedtime. It seemed alive, and when discussed, one expected it to join the conversation speaking in a slow and deep baritone.

Since school was out, Ruby had nothing to occupy her time but chores and day dreams about the reunion. She enjoyed having a good time, and she missed the family members who'd moved away to the big cities.

Ruby and her cousin Pearl had never been close, and she was the closest girl to her age in town. Ruby thought Pearl a goody-two-shoes, a church girl, a mama's baby.

Although they were only a few years apart, they were as different as day and night.

Secretly, Ruby envied Pearl. Her parents gave her everything she wanted. Aunt Lila was the easiest woman to talk to, and Uncle Mitchell had been everywhere; Ruby loved listening to his stories about life on the railroad.

Ever since her mother died she and Walker stayed with her aunt and uncle. Her father visited and made sure they had what they needed, but they never felt close to him and he never pushed for anything else. It was as if he had nothing left to give them.

Walker and Early, who everyone called "the boys," were both older than Ruby and not interested in having a sister and a girl cousin tag along with them everywhere they went.

Finally the big day of the reunion arrived. The first to arrive was Luther and his wife Katherine with Danny, who was just a year old and who already took after his father. They arrived late Thursday night; too late for Ruby to greet them, but she got up early the next morning and ran up the trail to where they were staying with Aunt Mozell and Joe. She was just in time for a country breakfast of fried fish, biscuits and molasses, grits and eggs.

The family talked, joked and laughed away the day with memories of earlier times. By late evening, when Junior and his family arrived, the reunion was well underway.

Saturday arrived along with Willa and her children, Tyrone and Rachel, and Iona and her son Mason. The group spread out between Lila and Mozell's house. A few of the men stayed with Hap. Although Lee lived in the large family home, no one suggested staying at the house on the mountain top and no one went up to visit with him.

Saturday night was the night set aside to throw a shindig for their friends. Everyone gathered at the picnic area the men cleared just for the occasion. The Fords, the Lathrops, the Turners – all family friends who had known each other so long not to have them at the reunion would have been like forgetting to invite your grandmother.

So many people came that Ruby couldn't keep up with them. She hung around the men folk who provided music for the group, playing guitars, harmonicas, and singing.

Occasionally Sis Turner would sing. She had the best voice and loved singing slow and melancholy songs like Bessie Smith's "Give me a Pig Foot and a Bottle of Beer" or anything by Billie Holiday.

Ruby, Pearl, Estelle Ford and Lillie Lathrop had babysitting duties. Danny was already asleep but the others were unmanageable. They sneaked away all the time, trying to steal sips of whiskey or homebrew from neglected glasses.

Finally Ruby slipped away too; staying just beyond the circle of singers and dancers, and away from the older women who gathered around the loaded food table, gossiping and laughing.

Lee, Odean, Hap and the older men sat around kerosene lamps drinking and talking over old times. They laughed at the good memories and grew silent after each unpleasant one. Hap would occasionally visit the circle where the younger men rolled dice, bragging about their gaming skills.

Ruby finally joined the group where her older cousins, Iona, Willa, Junior's wife Billie and Luther's wife Katherine gossiped with women their own age. The women included her in the conservation which revolved around children and work.

Ruby had other ideas and got Willa and Katherine talking about living in Detroit. She hung onto every word, visualizing herself in the big city dancing in fancy clubs dressed in clinging gowns, furs and rhinestones. Ruby couldn't wait to leave Alabama, to see the tall buildings called skyscrapers, and to have fun every night.

The shindig was a huge success. Everyone later said it was one of the best they could remember.

It was close to midnight when a brand new Chevrolet, hardly covered with dust, purred up the graveled road. The headlights moved over Ruby's body as she danced by herself to guitar music.

She had her eyes closed, so at first she did not know she was captured in the headlights, her young body moving in time with the guitar, hips thrusting to a blues tune. The light played over her body until she realized how silent everyone had become and opened her eyes.

The headlights dimmed and went out; everybody watched as the doors opened. Unknown strangers at a gathering usually meant trouble. A sigh rose from the group as Sandy Ford got out of the door on the passenger's side. A young man got out from the driver's side, closed the door, walked around to Sandy and put his arm around her waist. They stood and posed alongside the sleek black vehicle.

Sandy was beautiful in a yellow and black dress. Her clear skin and red lips were flushed from the excitement of a new car, a handsome man and Saturday night.

"Everybody, look at Rick's car! Ain't it just grand," she said.

All the young men and several of the older men crowded around the car. The young men danced around the car and the old men gazed upon its sleek beauty with envy. They asked questions: how fast could it go, how much did it cost and other such assorted male talk.

Rick Leslie was Sandy's boyfriend. Ruby couldn't take her eyes off his perfect features; his skin was like "just right" coffee, full lips covered by a pencil thin moustache, eyes like the car's headlights, bright and probing. When Sandy walked over to giggle and talk among her family and friends, Ruby moved closer to the road, to the car, to the man.

Sis Turner sang something fast and hot; just about everybody started dancing or moving to the beat. Ruby saw Uncle Mitchell swing Aunt Lila into his arms; they circled around the clearing like young lovers.

"Would you like to dance?"

Ruby turned to see Rick standing behind her, between her and an old elm tree. He had been watching her as she stood swaying in time to the music.

"Would you like to dance?" he asked again with his arms outstretched. Before she could think, he led her into the circle of other dancers. With his arm around her waist, he spun her into his embrace and out into the hot, southern night. Again and again, round and round. She felt dizzy and peaceful all at the same time.

Each time she was spun into his embrace she looked up into his handsome face. He had slanted, almond shaped eyes and a high forehead where curls lay like a crown upon his head. Each time she was spun out into the humid night, the absence of his long and lean body shocked her.

That night, in bed, Ruby concentrated intently on her body. It felt alien to her, as if something inside had woken up and wanted out.

She ached and throbbed until finally falling into a deep and heavy sleep.

Sunday morning the Ghee clan filled the pews of Second Baptist Church. Even Odean and EJ made a rare appearance. Pastor Crutcher beamed at everyone from the pulpit and prayed for their wellbeing and success.

Before leaving the old, white washed church, the family walked around back to the graveyard to visit with Preston, Jacob, Truly, Vesta, Thom, Lou, Essie, Marie and other deceased family members.

Theodore Jamerson, the Ghee patriarch, was buried in the white graveyard over in Teluchi.

Monday found the group headed into Huntsville for a visit to Junior's new club. He called it The Jaybird. After Jacob's tragic death, Junior closed the Joint and moved to Huntsville.

The sheriff was paid off and Reece Jones' body was never found. For six months Junior blamed himself and refused to consider opening another honky-tonk.

After months of working odd jobs and either quitting or getting fired after a few weeks, he realized operating a bar was what he did best. The Jaybird was located close to the Negro community, the highway and the Elks Lodge.

From the beginning, The Jaybird was a huge success. It was a step above the old place with a real bar that Junior swore was mahogany and a jukebox stocked with blues tunes. Now he even sold, to those who could afford it, store-bought whiskey, wine and beer.

Poker and crap games were played in a back room where Junior still sold homebrew and white lightening, mostly to his older customers. Big Top took up his position at the front door; a new sheriff stopped by every now and then for his cut and business was good.

The Jaybird was usually closed for business on Monday, but Junior opened the place up and treated his family to an evening of dancing. The smaller kids got left with a babysitter at Junior and Billie's house. Ruby was allowed to attend, along with Pearl, Walker and Early. She felt so grown up!

Luther and Willa were visiting The Jaybird for the first time, and they complimented Junior so much his round face shone with pride. Luther immediately started making suggestions about how to make more money at The Jaybird and other improvements.

All night long friends stopped by to visit. Junior's friends John, Nate and Seth came in and settled at two tables. Nate was with his wife Shirley, who was one of Billie's friends. John was with a short dark woman who popped gum all night. Seth started teasing Iona about when they were kids and how she used to be sweet on him when another group of well-wishers arrived.

Ruby glanced up in time to see Rick walk in with a group of Early's friends.

For once in her life, she was speechless. She'd been thinking about him ever since he'd climbed out of the black car and danced with her under the elm tree. She hoped to see him again, but did not know how to find out who he was or where he was.

Now he stood within a few feet of her. He looked good dressed all in black with a gold-colored belt around his waist holding up baggy pants that still seemed to fit him like a glove. His dark, thin moustache and conked hair glistened in the lights of Junior's bar.

Ruby smoothed down the dark green dress she wore, and then brushed the sides of her hair back in place. Her face felt shiny and she wondered if her lipstick needed a touch up.

Rick threw back his head and laughed at something Early said. It reminded Ruby of her father's deep baritone laugh. She shivered all the way down to her toes.

When he and the group of young men headed towards the back room, Ruby started after them but was stopped by a tap on her shoulder. It was EJ; she'd been watching Ruby watch Rick.

"Men don't like it when they women follow them all the time," EJ said as she blocked her way.

Ruby was ready with a quick reply when she realized what EJs' comment meant. It signified she could be his woman! The sharp reply died on her lips and she gazed after the young men as they disappeared into the back room, closing the door after them.

"Come on now. Sit down with me a spell. Let's talk." EJ led Ruby to a far corner of the bar, away from the noise, the dancing and the kinfolk.

"I ain't the only one been noticing how you looking at that boy. Your Aunt Lila notice, and if I hadn't stopped you from going off after him she woulda."

Ruby glanced over to look at Lila. Mozell and several other women sat and chatted with her over drinks. Sure enough her aunt looked at her with a startled expression on her face. She appeared to notice for the first time that Ruby was no longer the little girl crying for her mama that she took in on that awful night when she and EJ found two women stabbed to death.

"But I'm not a baby anymore," Ruby said aloud and sat down.

"True, you ain't. But you ain't quite a woman yet either." EJ took a big swig of her drink that made her eyes water.

She'd been sick awhile back and lost a lot of weight. Her fleshy arms wobbled as she sat down the glass.

"Now, we can talk, if you want. If you don't want to talk to me I suggest you talk to your aunt. 'Cause if you don't get somebody's advice on what you about to do you gonna be in a heap of trouble." EJ glanced around the room, noticing that Odean looked happy but tired.

"It's just that I ain't got anything to do living in the country. Ain't no other girls my age close enough for me to visit with, and Pearl and I don't exactly get along with each other." Ruby did feel better talking to EJ and realized this was their first grown-up talk together.

"Is that it? What about this boy, ain't he courting that Ford girl?"

"Yeah, I guess. First time I saw him was two days ago when they come to the shindig."

"He's a lot older than you are. I don't think your daddy gone care for him to come calling on you." Even as EJ said it, she could see Ruby did not take the comment well at all.

Ruby tossed her head back and lightning seemed to flash from her eyes. She stood up from the table and placed her hands on her hips. At that moment EJ glimpsed the woman Ruby would become; she was shocked that she didn't care for her at all.

"I'm old enough and if y'all don't think so it's too bad."

EJ watched her walk away like a determined lioness on the prowl.

For Ruby, the rest of the week passed without any additional chances to see Rick again.

Tuesday, the family drove to Guntersville Lake to fish and picnic all day. Wednesday, the group separated. All the women but Lila, who'd had to return to work, drove into Decatur for some shopping.

The men decided to take it easy, which meant they would mostly sleep before heading back to The Jaybird.

Thursday was hair day. The women took turns washing, straightening and curling each other's hair, while getting ready for the final days together.

Ruby had chores to do and didn't make it down to her Aunt Mozell's house until late afternoon when she was scheduled to fix Willa's hair. She walked into Mozell's house amidst the aroma of burnt hair, Royal Crown hairdressing and moon pies. Mozell loved moon pies and ate them all the time. When it was hot you could always smell chocolate and marshmallow in her house.

Ruby had taken the long way around, first going down The Hollow trail to check the mailboxes located down off the main road where the old grocery store use to be. Now the store had collapsed. Only one wall remained standing and kudzu choked all remnants of what had been a thriving business.

She also stopped off at the pigpen to check on the newest litter of piglets. She wasn't fond of the nasty animals, but she'd been promised the pick of the litter to fatten up all summer and sell come slaughter time.

She'd taken the long way around and that's why she had to enter the house through the front door, which was closest to the road, instead of the back door, which was where the kitchen was.

She stopped just inside the screen door next to a wooden stand topped off by a glass dish that Joe used as an ashtray. His favorite chair, a dark blue, stuffed armchair that Mozell had patched and stitched up over a dozen times, stood next to the ashtray stand.

No one heard Ruby come in and when she heard what the women were talking about she didn't call out so they'd know she was there. She stayed just out of eyesight but not out of hearing distance.

"I say he killed Auntie Lou!" Iona was near tears.

"But I thought they killed themselves," Katherine said.

"Baby, don't go and get upset. It was a long time ago," Mozell advised Iona. "And, we don't know what all happened. Ain't that right, Lila?"

"Too many things happen 'round here nobody know nothing about. That's one reason why I left," Willa sounded just as upset as Iona.

"Mama, you OK?" Pearl asked Lila.

"Sure, baby. All this talking about things that can't be undone makes me sad," Lila answered.

"What if you could do something?" Iona hissed.

"Maybe this ain't something we should be talking about right now," Mozell said. She combed Katherine's hair, sectioning off parts of the hair as she ran the straightening comb between each section. After each run through of the comb the hair relaxed into an unnatural straight texture.

Mozell's face was wet with sweat and sweat rings formed underneath her armpits. "We should continue this another time."

"But we are not babies!" Pearl yelled. Lila grabbed and tickled her; the sound of her laughter cut through the gloom somewhat. Iona wiped her face with a towel and smiled at the young woman who squirmed in her mother's arms.

For a while, no one spoke. Finally Mozell started talking about one of her favorite topics – food. Katherine asked her for several recipes which Mozell was happy to provide.

When the group discussed things again in a normal fashion, Ruby started to go out and come back in the front door as if she'd just arrived. As she turned, the homemade ashtray stand fell over, spilling cigarette butts and ashes all over the floor.

"Oh, no, I've made a mess; hello everybody," Ruby announced, bending at once to collect the ashtray trash and to hide her face from the group as they rushed to assist her.

Lila searched her face for clues that she'd overheard the conversation. When their eyes met, Lila knew that she had. One day soon they would have to talk. It was time to share family secrets.

The summer was endless. Ruby had little to occupy her time, but determined as ever, she made future plans.

Two years after meeting the man she loved, Ruby started working weekends and holidays at The Jaybird. She'd convinced her aunt and father that she needed to make some money if she planned to go to college, that it would be easier to attend high school in Huntsville so she could work at the bar.

She still remembered the joy on their faces when she started talking about attending Alabama A&M. Lila promised to save everything she could to help Ruby with the expenses. Thinking about it now made Ruby feel guilty. She'd never intended going to college; the only thing she thought about was Rick.

Lee seemed suspicious from the beginning. He and Odean had friends everywhere; Ruby didn't want them to find out she was going out with Rick before she was ready. But it was worth it! The moments she spent with him, usually in the backseat of his Ford, were precious to her.

Working at The Jaybird was hard work. Junior was tough and demanding; because Ruby was his cousin, she had expected smooth sailing. She dared not complain because this was the only chance she had to see Rick.

They were supposed to get together later tonight.

Ruby never stayed at work until the bar closed. Junior didn't want her out at all hours of the night. She usually got off at 9 o'clock and would drive Billie's car back to the house. Most nights Billie and the children were either already asleep or on the way to dreamland. After a few hours she would slip out and wait for Rick.

She took an order for rum and Coke and glanced at her watch and was surprised to see it was ten minutes to nine. Ruby ran to the bar, nearly tripping over Big Top's size 12 feet. She gave her final order of the night to Junior's bartender, a glum man named Wesley.

Fifteen minutes later Ruby exceeded the speed limit driving to her cousin's house. She needed to freshen up, change clothes and comb her hair before she saw her man.

Driving up the alley, Ruby noticed a car similar to Rick's black Chevy turn into the Elks Lodge parking lot. She was in a hurry so she kept going, thinking only of what dress to wear so she'd look good for him. Later, she would remember seeing the car and thinking that it could be him.

Careful not to make noises that would wake the sleeping family, Ruby tipped around the silent house to the room she shared with the baby. A quick glance at the clock on the dresser told her to hurry. It was already 10 o'clock. Rick said he would pick her up at 10:30.

Tonight would be their first real date! Rick promised to take her out to a place in Tennessee.

Everything needed to be perfect. Tonight she wanted to talk about their future. She had a secret and tonight it was time to reveal that secret.

Sitting down in front of the dresser, Ruby looked at herself in the large round mirror. Her hair was tied back with a black scarf. She removed the scarf and ran her fingers through her hair. Looking into the mirror, she applied bright red lipstick and gathered her hair and twisted it into a bun on top of her head. Using hair pins to secure it, Ruby decided Rick would think it looked sexy.

To complete the look, she selected a gold brocade dress, brought with some of the money from her job at The Jaybird. She'd gone shopping with Billie, who had been surprised at her purchase of the dress and had tried to talk her out of buying it. Billie, and everyone else, thought she saved money for college.

They would all soon know her plan; it was all part of the surprise.

The gold dress fit her like a glove. It clung to her small body and caressed her curves like Rick's hands. She smiled at the thought of those hands circling her tiny waist, cupping her breasts and pulling her into his hard embrace. Whew! She sat down and powdered her perfect face and applied more lipstick.

One final look in the mirror and she knew she looked better than ever.

Junior hummed off-key to "Blues Knocking," Jacob's song, as he pulled into his driveway about 1 o'clock that Sunday morning.

The bar had made more money tonight than ever before. In fact, things went so well, he'd had a drink and left early. He didn't usually drink at his own establishment. Well, not since Jacob was killed anyway.

Singing his late brother's song and now thinking about their last time together made Junior sad. He parked his car and sat for a minute, listening to the engine make ticking,

164

cooling down sounds and remembering Jacob. Inside the car, just a few minutes before, he'd been happy and filled with a sense of prosperity; now a sense of forbearing settled in.

So, seeing Ruby was not a surprise. She walked in front of the car and stood looking at him; a bedraggled thing in a wrinkled gold dress, hair standing out all over her head, makeup smeared across her face. But it was her eyes that scared him; he saw madness looking back at him.

*   *   *   *

Most of them could never recall a family gathering at Lee's house. So they, mostly the young men who strutted around the old fashioned furniture like panthers on the prowl, were uneasy. The older men sat around the kitchen table, sipping whiskey or coffee, waiting for Lee to indicate how they would handle the situation.

The women gathered in the parlor. Tears and angry words had given way to sadness and finally a weary acceptance that this was the way of things. Girls got pregnant, many times without a husband.

Ruby lay down in one of the cluttered bedrooms, listening to the confined whispers of the women, the impotent shuffling of the old men around the kitchen table, and the impatient prowling of the young men from the living room.

Earlier Pearl sat at the foot of the bed and attempted consoling conversation. When Ruby would not respond she'd given up and joined the other women. Ruby knew that they were all truly concerned and wanted to help; maybe Pearl wanted to build a better relationship with her cousin. But all Ruby could think about was Rick.

She could not believe the things they said about him. Rick was seeing Sandy while he kept Ruby on the side. Pearl said everyone expects him to marry Sandy. Daddy said their child would be raised without a father. Ruby knew that he loved her and she would not listen to them any longer.

Rising from the bed, Ruby paced around, keeping in time with the prowling sounds which continued to come from the living room. She was impatient to see Rick. He said he loved her. Surely this was all a mistake.

She needed to see him, to talk to him and share her secret. Her family knew she was pregnant but she'd not had the opportunity to let him know. Once he knew about the baby, everything would be alright. They could get married and it would all be perfect.

She had to see him.

Ruby spotted the gold brocade dress draped over a chair by the bed. The keys to Billie's car were still in one of the rumpled dress pockets.

"It ain't like he forced her," in the kitchen Lee finally spoke.

"Say what!" Odean responded in dismay.

166

"She say she been goin' out to him," was Lee's defense.

"Yea, but he know what he doing," Odean shouted. "He's older and more experienced."

"He should take some responsibility," Mitchell stated, as ever the mediator.

"But he been seeing that Ford girl," Junior reminded his uncles. "Ain't that right, Walker?"

The young cousins heard the discussion and now stood in the doorway. They were a mass of unleashed tension, but hesitated to make a full commitment until they knew for sure what was expected of them. Ruby was blood; Rick was just a friend, someone they went out with to have a good time. So, they hung back with their comments, waiting for Walker to speak for them as one.

"That's right, never said anything about Ruby," Walker finally spoke. "Damn, this ain't right!"

"Wait a minute, Ruby ain't the one we talking about," Odean stood up and slammed his fist down on the old oak table. "We talking 'bout a man who done got an innocent girl in trouble."

The outburst ended with a coughing spell that bent Odean's frail body over with pain. Raw, racking coughs silenced the conversation. They waited for the spell to subside. Odean reached into his back pocket and pulled out a handkerchief; when he coughed into the blue and white piece of cotton, reddish spittle covered his lips. He wiped his mouth and teary eyes.

Looking into the shocked eyes around the table, shrugging off Lee's hand on his shoulder, Odean straightened up and continued his comments.

"It's alright, been living like this for a spell and gone live with it a little longer. Best thing could happen to me now is that we handle this like Ghee men. I gotta piss. When I get back, I expect to hear ya'll talkin' about what we gonna do for Ruby."

Odean walked down the shotgun hallway, reaching into his overall pocket for a cigarette. He didn't need to pee; he just wanted to clear his head. How could this have happen to his darling Ruby?

Just before he lit the Winston dangling between his lips, he saw movement by the side of the house by the cars. He put his hand in his pocket and went as quickly as he could toward the movement. Even out here you couldn't be too careful, might be someone up to no good he thought as he tried to get closer and get a better view.

The figure by the car jumped in surprise and turned around; it was Ruby!

"Girl, what you doing out here?" Odean released his hand on the gun in his pocket and hurried toward his niece.

"Ya'll can't stop me, I need to see Rick!" Ruby backed up against the car, clutching the keys to her chest. She ran around to the driver's side, opened the door and got inside the car. Odean reached the passenger's side and slide in as the car slammed forward into the dark southern night.

The car flew down country roads as fast as thoughts flew around in her head. Odean finally stopped trying to talk her out of looking for Rick. He had settled into the passenger's seat, occasionally smoking a cigarette and coughing.

They had checked out all the usual late night hangouts; all the joints in Morgan County. But he was nowhere to be found. The only places left were in the city.

Ruby made a left turn at the Wavaho Gas Station at the corner of Highway 54 and Spring Road and started the car across the two lane bridge. Where should they go first? She realized that the only places she could think to look for him were clubs and bars; most of which she'd only seen from the parking lot as he met with other men or went in and came back out to bring her a BBQ sandwich or a drink.

By the time she reached the city, her heart thumped around in her chest like a caged animal. Her whole body flooded with relief when she didn't see the black Ford parked in the lot of the VFW club. She wanted to find him, but not at a place where everyone would see her come looking for her man.

In a near panic she drove across the Veterans Parkway to the Elks lodge. At this late hour the club was just about empty; but a popular local group had performed earlier and the club had been filled to capacity. Men and women still lingered in the lot chatting with friends and gossiping about the night's earlier activities.

All of the women were older than Ruby, and she thought they looked better as well. Jewels flashed in the headlights of the parked cars, their hair was salon maintained instead of a kitchen fix-up, nails long, pointed and blood red.

The men were attractive and dressed as fine as Rick in two-tone Stacey Adams shoes, suits in colors of plum, green and blue to highlight their slick black hair and thin mustaches.

Ruby drove through the parking lot, all the while looking for Rick. She started calling out to those who passed by. 'Have you seen Rick Leslie tonight?' Most of the club goers had not. Finally, one young man who wore a hat the same deep shade of burgundy as his suit said that he'd seen him a few hours ago at the Dew Drop.

The information made her impatient to be with him, Ruby sped forward honking the car horn to urge the revelers to make way.

"There it is!" Ruby yelled with relief and excitement when she saw Rick's car. "There's no place to park. I'll have to park on the street. But don't worry Uncle Odean, I'll be leaving with Rick tonight and you can drive the car back to Junior and Billie's house."

Ruby parked and adjusted the rearview mirror for a quick look at her face. The woman in the rearview mirror was a stranger with hollow eyes, disheveled hair and smeared makeup. Ruby only thought about how it would feel to be held by Rick once again. She stepped outside the car, forgetting Odean in her hurry to get inside the club.

"Wait a minute, baby, let's talk about how things should happen when you see him." Odean was by her side and took her arm. Ruby turned around. She was ready to yell at him to leave her alone, but for the moment she saw that he was a tired, sick old man. He'd been silent during most of the ride, coughing every now and then, keeping her company during the long night. She waited for him to have his say, ready to agree to anything just as long as she could hurry to Rick.

"I know you excited, findin' him and all." Odean paused, looking at the troubled young woman. "But you got to realize that he might not be excited to see you."

"What you mean!" Despite all her earlier restraint, a sudden temper sprang up in her at his words.

"No, don't get me wrong; let's think about how to get his attention." Odean desperately wanted to find Rick before Ruby did. "Suppose he's in there gambling, you think he want you rushing in and spoiling a winning streak?"

His words made sense. Ruby calmed down but continued towards the club door. Odean followed, begging her to let him go in first. She finally gave in to the arrangements and told him she'd give him five minutes before coming in to find both him and Rick. Odean hurried inside, determined to find the man and make him do his duty.

Ruby waited outside, already guessing how the club would be laid out. A long bar would be against one side of the room, a collection of mismatched tables and chairs would occupy the center of the room and a space small enough to hold a trio of musicians would be across from the front door. A small kitchen and bathroom would be on the opposite side of the box-shaped room.

The Dew Drop didn't disappoint. When finally she entered the door exactly five minutes later, a huge block of a man, the peacekeeper, looked her up and down as she stepped inside the dim, smoky room. Ruby moved quickly to the left, giving her eyes a chance to adjust to the room and hoping to spot Rick before he saw her.

A blues tune played from the jukebox; it was a song she didn't recognize. Tonight the club didn't appear to have a live band.

Across the room Ruby saw John, one of Junior's friends. His back was turned to her but she knew that if she wasn't careful someone who knew her family would see her and come over asking all kinds of nosy questions.

There was one place where she couldn't be seen; in the hallway leading to the toilet. It was on the side of the room closest to where she was standing. She would not have to cross the room where everybody could see her.

Ruby entered the hallway where she could smell the odor of stale cigarettes, liquor and perfume and also the stink from the toilet. At least she had a fairly good view.

Quite a few of the people in the room were also regulars at The Jaybird. In addition to John and his girlfriend Faye there were the Lyman twins, and Ruby saw Sandy sitting at a table filled with other women. Ruby wanted to go over and sit with her because Sandy might know where Rick was tonight. She was one of his friends and at one time they were courting. Ruby hesitated; If Sandy knew about the baby she might lie and give false information.

There was still no sign of Rick and now Ruby didn't see Odean either.

Ruby made up her mind and started across the crowded room. She weaved in and out of tables filled with drunken people; ignoring the few who called her name and inquired after family members. Halfway to Sandy's table she felt a pinch on her rear end and almost stopped to slap the fool who did it into next Sunday, but that's when she saw Rick.

He looked so good. He wore a dark blue suit that made him look like a movie star.

Ruby ran across the room, pushing people out of her way until she could fling herself into Rick's arms. She closed her eyes as she hugged him with all her strength. It felt peaceful in his arms and she was happy. She'd come looking for Rick and she'd found him.

When she opened her eyes and looked at him, he seemed surprised to see her.

Ruby felt her hair being pulled. She was torn from Rick's arms and flung onto the cigarette littered, nasty floor. Sandy stood over her with her hands on her hips, legs spread wide and murder on her face.

"Why you little heifer!" Sandy yelled down at her. "What you think you doing jumping all over my man, ain't you got no respect!"

Ruby watched with amazement as Rick pulled on Sandy's arm, pulling her away from Ruby as she still lay sprawled across the stinking floor. She concentrated hard to hear what they were saying as Sandy fought him off, waiting to attack Ruby if she attempted to get up off the floor.

"Now, baby, don't get yourself upset!" Rick said. He never once looked down at Ruby. "Let's go baby. Odean is here and he can take care of Ruby. He'll make sure she gets back home where she belongs."

Odean bent down, helping Ruby stand up, talking to her telling her it was time to go, that she'd found Rick and he wasn't worth her time.

Sandy allowed herself to be coaxed away. Ruby stood shivering with shock, Odean's arms wrapped around her.

"Everybody wait one damn minute!" Ruby found her voice and flung it as high as she could. Every eye in the club turned to watch her as she painfully walked toward the couple. The whites of her eyes had turned red with rage, her hair stood on end around her head like a static cloud, her ashen face sweated under the dim lights of the club.

"I got your baby inside me and you allow another woman to fling me around like I'm filth! Should I tell her what you whisper in my ear as you make love to me! You said you loved me, told me I was your woman, you my man . . ." tears slid down her sunken cheeks.

Ruby stood trembling before the couple, shamed that she had ever loved him. She had not listened to her family

174

and friends, and now she had to recognize the truth: he didn't want her, probably never had.

"You are a liar and a whore and without honor." Ruby addressed Rick but her raw emotions filled the room. "I hope you go to hell and never come back!'

"You want him Sandy? Well, I hope you never get away from him. He will wear you down and wear you out." Ruby's last comment followed the couple as they left the club.

Ruby, sobbing and tearing at her hair, slowly made her way to the door. Odean followed Ruby, attempting to soothe her with words that even to him felt empty. He followed her to the car and couldn't stop her before she got into the driver's side. He got in on the passenger's side.

"Baby, you got to see that you deserve better than him," Odean said as he fumbled in his overall pocket searching for a handkerchief. "We'll take care of you and the baby."

He gave up the search and turned his niece's face toward him and wiped away the tears, sweat and snot with his calloused hands. He made soothing sounds to her and searched her face for any sign of reason. Her bloodshot eyes stared back at him. The pupils' looked through and past him to a private misery.

A few hours later, a blue car drove along the back country roads; at times roaring along as if the final destination was a long way off and it had to get there in time for some celebration or emergency. Other times, the car stopped from time to time along the dirt roads as if looking for something lost perhaps from a previous visit.

The roads were dark and from a distance an owl hooted and kept track of the car's passing by swiveling its head until the headlights faded away. The blue car continued on around another bend and turn in the road. Speeding again, it smashed into a metal mailbox perched atop a wooden stake driven into the hard dirt at the side of the road.

Years of inclement weather, high winds and impatient mail carriers had already loosened the wooden stake's grip on solid ground. The impact sent the wooden post and mailbox rocketing skyward. The stake landed harmlessly in the dirt yard of Herb and Millie Evans, sole occupants of rural route #78.

The mailbox landed on the Evans' tin roof, bounced once and slid down the other side of the roof into a rain barrel Herb kept against the side of the house. The commotion woke up Herb and the family's dog; Millie kept on snoring.

The car continued, zigzagging across the road as if unable to make up its mind to go to the left or to the right, right or left. Then it straightened out and continued on into the darkness.

Five miles ahead the one lane bridge crossed the Chickamauga River. But the blue car missed the narrow road and drove off the embankment on the left side of the bridge, plunging headfirst into the cold, muddy river waters. The car floated on the river's surface. An eruption of bubbles rose around the car.

Just before the car slid downward and out of sight, two figures popped to the surface; one figure towed the other slowly towards the bank. The figures disappeared once, slipping under the water, but the one who towed the still and silent figure was determined and endured until both reached the safety of the river's Ledge. He pulled, pushed and dragged until finally he could do no more and collapsed after one last attempt to ensure his companion was on dry ground.

"Want bird. Bird Fly. Want bird."

The man carried me toward a large house with a porch. I held my hands out for the bird, which even as I spoke took flight and escaped across the brilliant blue sky. The blue, red, yellow colors all excited my two-year-old mind. Even then I wanted to escape with the bird into the unknown.

I kept on crying but the man marched onward toward the house and mama's waiting arms.

"Hush, now, hush." Mama grabbed for me and her arms closed around my squirming body.

"What's wrong, what did you do," she questioned.

I babbled about the bird with the pretty colors, but mama put me on her hip, holding me to one side as she spat angry words at the man who stood in the doorway. Somehow I knew they would continue to argue for a while, so I continued to squirm until mama released me.

Unnoticed, I ran off down the hallway to a room with roses on the wall where my prized possession waited. Her name was Dolly. Her round plastic head held two vivid blue eyes, fringed by uneven lashes that closed when you lay her down. Well, one eye closed, you had to open and close the other when you changed her position.

Her hair used to be blond; now it was purple (I shampooed it with blackberry preserves).

The angry sounds moved away from my safe place. They were now just next door, in the kitchen. I heard loud noises, as if they were moving around the table or chairs; playing some adult game that only they knew the rules to.

Mama screamed a lot.

I told Dolly that we had to keep quiet. I told Dolly that I would change her clothes and we would play games for a while. I talked to Dolly a long time that day, longer than I had ever talked to her. She seemed to understand everything.

Finally the man came to get me. He sat me on his lap to tell me a story. I'd heard it before; I didn't like it very much. I wanted my mama but she didn't come.

*   *   *   *

The school bus was never reliable and broke down at least once every school year, stranding the children and Fred Gaines, the old bus driver, by the side of the road. Sometimes it broke down in a populated area and sometimes, like today, it died in an area no one was liable to pass by in a long time.

Eight-year-old Honor Ghee, two other children and Mr. Gaines were stranded off Route 36 and Morgan County Highway in Teluchi; the other two children had only a short walk to get home. Debbie and "Booger" Green lived within a mile or so of where the old school bus had broken down.

Honor would have to walk at least a mile just to get to Vermosa and at least another mile before she reached The Hollow and home.

She set out on the highway and within a short distance turned off onto a well-traveled path towards the old trail up the mountain. Her small figure moved determinedly forward, thin legs moving briskly, lunch sack in one hand and a book bag in the other; she looked neither to the right nor the left.

Honor didn't mind the walk; nothing much else to do when you lived in the country. Jennifer Wilson was her nearest friend and she lived several miles away from Honor. She was only worried that she'd get home late ..... Aunt Lila wasn't feeling too well these days. In the wintertime, she said she had arthritis and her joints ached. Today was cold and dreary. Honor would be lucky if it didn't rain before she got home.

Honor knew that when she got home Aunt Lila would be wrapped in a quilt sitting by the stove drinking a hot cup of her favorite tea – sassafras. She'd always have a smile for Honor no matter how bad her joints ached. Uncle Mitchell passed away last year; cousins Early and Pearl no longer lived at home, and Honor knew her aunt looked forward to her companionship.

Besides, she loved her Aunt Lila and living with her was better than times she spent with her mother. Ruby was hard to please and even harder to get along with. Honor tried hard to do everything she could but she could do nothing right. Whenever she saw Ruby, or for the brief times Ruby settled down long enough for child welfare to consider it a home, something always went wrong.

Her mother struggled throughout life. She was erratic at best, gambling, drinking, staying out and never working long at any job.

She also had long periods of depression where she lay in bed all day and just drank whatever was available. Honor tried to take care of her during these dark periods. She brushed her hair, gave her sponge baths and fed her whatever she could find. When nothing was available, she went to neighbors or called on family for help.

She hated this part of The Hollow. The mountain was dressed in the dark gray, black and soot colors of winter. Yet the colors seemed to never change on parts of the mountain. No matter the weather, these areas in particular always seemed to be in mourning.

Honor had heard stories of crazy Lou, who was her grandfather's first wife, and how she had killed her baby and went mad roaming these mountains looking for it. There was also the story of Aunt Lila's first child, baby Truly, who had been dragged into the river by a giant water moccasin and never seen again.

Honor knew there was some truth to the stories and each time she thought about them she always had a picture of the mountain in the background, as if it waited for an opportunity for things to go wrong ..... Perhaps even eager for things to go wrong.

She shivered inside her red and black checkered winter coat and increased her speed on the old trail hoping to make it home before the sun went down. That was not a good thought, being out after dark at the top of the mountain ......

Thinking of those old stories put her on edge. She welcomed a peep from a bird or any sound to let her know that the mountain creatures had not yet settled down inside their burrows for the long night and she was not out here alone.

Honor made her way forward; her warm breath puffing out behind her like smoke until she came to the top of the mountain. She looked out over The Hollow below her. She couldn't see all the way down to the old store her grandfather and his brothers had owned when they were young men, or to her Aunt Lila's house but she thought she saw smoke coming from that direction.

To her left, one of Miz Dora's relatives rented out a cabin; another old cabin in the distance had caved in many years ago.

Just ahead of her she could pick out the family house where her grandfather still lived. Funny, they still called it the family house after all these years. It had once been her home. Her mother Ruby, Grandma Essie and, of course, her grandfather all lived there before she was born.

Honor did not want to walk past the house but on this part of the old trail that was the only way down to the other side. She was never comfortable in her grandfather's presence and Aunt Lila never wanted her to spend much time alone with him.

A powerful memory of her mother floated to her mind. It was from the time she stayed with Ruby before child welfare took her out of her care….the first time.

She had been left alone in the dirty, one bedroom apartment she shared with Ruby in the projects; she was only two years old. Neighbors listened to her cries for two days before finally calling the police. Grandfather came to the county's family social services office and claimed her and took her to live with Aunt Lila until Ruby returned.

But there were other memories; a blue bird or Blue Jay that flew close enough to reach out and touch it. And, of course, all the times she played with her favorite doll, Dolly..........

Something moved through the dense forest on her left. At first it blended in with the fall colors of russet, gold and deep red until grandfather stepped onto the path. He had on an old gold and red plaid flannel shirt; his broad and calloused hands shoved into the pockets of faded and tattered overalls.

"Hey baby. Why you walkin' home all by yourself?" He asked and smiled at me. When he smiled, he looked just like my mother; they had the same eyes. I smiled back.

"That old raggedly school bus done broke down again and Mr. Gaines didn't know how to fix it," I said, and thinking of all the times in the past we had to walk home, I got mad all over again.

"Gurl, don't frown like that. I've heard tell that when you frown the frown gets stuck on your face." Grandfather screwed his face up and made a giant frown between his eyes. He laughed a big, belly laugh that shook him all over. I laughed too.

"Want me to walk down the path with you." He said it as a statement and turned and started walking in the direction of Aunt Lila's house.

"Oh, no, that's OK. I'm just about home now." I turned to go around him but he just stood in the middle of the path.

"OK, but do me a favor. I dug up some sassafras roots a few months back and I know how much Lila love to make it into a tea and sometimes she uses it in somethin' a little stronger." This time he rocked back on his heels as he laughed his big, belly laugh. "Shoot, I could use somethin' stronger myself now that winter's settin' in."

Grandfather smacked his lips in appreciation of some of Aunt Lila's special home brews made with all kinds of dried fruits and secret flavorings that only she and Aunt Iona knew how to prepare.

I watched him turn and walk towards the family house; for just a second he turned his head back to me on the path and said to come on, that he already had the sassafras roots in a bag and it wouldn't take long to find it.

I hesitated just a second but soon started up the path behind grandfather

Section Three

THE FIRE NEXT TIME

The family house looked the same to me from long ago memories. It was a shotgun house with a front porch that now sagged so completely on one end it had completely collapsed into the foundation.

Inside to the left was the parlor with some remnants of great grandmother Vesta's once finer furnishings; now either faded or, like the front porch, sagging and or worn out completely. To the right was another room; a rocker and a side table were still in fairly good shape but all was covered with dust.

"Come on out back to the kitchen, Honor," grandfather called from the back of the house.

I made my way down the long hallway, looking into each of the bedrooms as I walked. One of the bedrooms was packed with boxes of who knew what, old and broken furniture, clothes so moldy that no one would want to go through them to salvage anything. Piles of paper stood around the room in danger of collapsing in a strong breeze. A sewing machine stood in one corner.

Something appeared to move in a far corner and I hurried along so I would not have to see if it was what I thought it might be. I was deathly afraid of rats and I did not want to hang around to see if that's what it could be.

Grandfather no longer kept the trees, vines and flowers on his property cut back. The house was now completely enclosed by greenery; so much so that the fading light outside did nothing to lighten up the dusty rooms. Only a small glow appeared at the back of the house; I smelled the odor of kerosene.

Before entering the kitchen I turned into the room on the right where I had stayed as a baby. There were signs here that this was now the room grandfather used; a messy bed was pushed against one wall, a maple chifferobe without handles was stuffed with shirts and overalls that spilled out onto the floor, a sofa covered with a quilt and a large side table with a radio occupied the rest of the room.

But it was the faded wallpaper that caught my attention. Large flowers that Aunt Lila called cabbage roses decorated the walls. I felt as if I could smell their aroma, as if I were in a garden and not a sad, old man's room. From memory, I saw myself in this room with a doll that had blue hair.

"Honor?" Grandfather called again from the kitchen. I shut off the long ago memories and hurried to the back of the house.

The kitchen table dominated the room, covered by what appeared to be the same oilcloth from so many years ago. On the table were the usual kitchen items, salt and pepper, hot sauce bottle, dirty dishes and a large glass bowl with half smoked cigar butts and one that still smoldered as if waiting for the next puff.

Grandfather rummaged around the back of the kitchen, mumbling that the bag was somewhere around here. I looked around at the disorder and offered to help him look for it and suggested we might be able to find it if we had more light in the room.

He grunted in agreement and found another kerosene lamp and lit the wick with a match from a Watkins tin.

"OK, you take this lamp and see if you find the bag in the cupboards over there," grandfather said, pointing to the right of the refrigerator. "I'ma take the other one and keep lookin' under the washstand. I know it's around here."

"Why we using the lamps, grandfather?" I asked as I pulled out one of the kitchen chairs to stand on to search the cabinets.

"Well, baby, you know I kind of let the electric wires fall into disrepair. Somewhere out there they just ain't active no more." Grandfather's voice appeared to be closer than when he last spoke. I turned and looked over my shoulder and he stood just behind me now with the kerosene lamp in one hand as he scratched his head with the other hand.

"Oh, but all you have to do is let the TVA people know that the wires are down and they'll come fix them. Aunt Lila had a problem last year and she had that white man that sell the insurance contact them for her and they came out within a week or two and took care of it."

I continued searching the last cabinet when I felt him put his hand on my leg. Thinking he thought I needed help getting down, I turned to tell him that I was OK.

Grandfather stood behind me and his hand was still on my leg. I looked into his eyes. The eyes that looked back at me were the eyes of my mother, but this time they also

188

reminded me of Teddy, one of the older boys at school who flirted with the older girls. I had seen him rub up against the girls and laugh when they pushed him away.

Grandfather's eyes now also reminded me of Mr. Riley, the white man who owned the farmland on the other side of The Hollow. Mr. Riley looked at all the colored women and girls with just that glazed and intent stare.

"Grandfather?"

He didn't answer but ran his hand up the inside of my leg even farther until his hand could not go any farther. He smiled.

"Noooo!"

Unconsciously I hit him on the head with the kerosene lamp I still held in my left hand. Hot oil spilled over his face and plaid flannel shirt; some spilled on my arm as well. He yelled and jumped back, dropping the lamp he carried as well.

The flame ignited the kerosene and the fire spread to grandfather. It ran up his pant leg and his shirt caught fire. He stumbled into the kitchen table and shoved it out of his way. The table landed against the hallway door, blocking the exit.

Grandfather ran around the kitchen looking for something to put out the fire. He grabbed me and pulled me off the chair where I still stood in frozen shock and disbelief. I pushed him away and the flame ignited the kerosene on my shirt and it began to burn. The pain overrode my shock and I started screaming. I ran to the hallway, but the table blocked the door.

The fire had spread up the walls to the roof. Grandfather tried to get out the back door. The door was stuck and refused to open. He couldn't get out and collapsed on the floor, jerking and screaming until finally he lay still. His entire body was on fire.

I turned back to the table which had just caught fire. Instinct told me to grab one of the kitchen chairs and with it in place I climbed over the table and escaped into the hallway.

My arm was on fire. I smelled the odor of burning Dixie Peach hair grease; my hair was on fire too. I raced down the hallway pulling at my hair, burning my hands and spreading the fire over the rest of my body. Overhead, fire flowed like an upside down river on the ceiling

The roar of the fire kept me company in the burning house, in the woods outside the house and along the trail that I'd walked all my life; it followed me all the way to Aunt Lila's front door.

BURNT BEANS

Honor's boss made a pass at her. Standing by Henry Garth's desk discussing the department's midyear budget requests she felt his hand on the back of her leg. It made her break out in a light sweat and the scars on her left arm and scalp itch, but she ignored the questing hand and moved around to the front of his desk and continued her discussion about furniture and equipment allocations. She needed the job.

Back in her office, Honor slumped at her cluttered desk and considered her choices. She should have slapped him – OK, then what? The question was addressed to an acrylic framed photo of her nine year-old daughter. It was a close-up shot and Rosie's smile filled the frame like sunshine. Honor swiveled in her chair, turning away from that bright smile; it made her feel like a coward.

Who was she kidding, for God's sake? She didn't have a college degree; she was 27 years old and a single parent. It might take months or a year to find another job in the depressed job market.

The window behind Honor's desk looked out over an alley filled with industrial trash cans, litter and a street person taking a siesta in a doorway. Across from her window, plump breasted pigeons strutted and cooed along the ledge of the building next door. Beyond the alley, Southern California sun shined eternal upon the cars and pedestrians that choked Ocean Boulevard.

Honor made it through the afternoon. She didn't see the trash or traffic outside her small office as she juggled her indecisions, mid-year budget figures and the beginnings of what promised to be a major headache.

Her boss's hand on her leg dredged up a memory of the fire that almost killed her and did kill her grandfather. Those memories always gave her a headache.

When she got home after work, Honor parked, locked and stood beside her battered VW. Outside of her apartment building, a black Toyota pickup cruised down the street. Inside the pickup a bald headed black teenage boy with an earring in one ear had his arm around a pretty but heavily made up Hispanic girl. The boy's right hand cupped and caressed the girl's breast; the girl giggled.

"I've got to get Rosie out of this neighborhood," Honor thought for what seemed like the millionth time, "or else she'll wind up dating punks like that."

As the truck slid past, music thumped and throbbed the Southern California evening like an abscessed tooth. Honor saw that some of the letters in the manufacturer's name had been painted over on back of the pickup. "YO" the truck proclaimed as it clunked down Elm Street.

Glancing after the truck with disdain, Honor walked across the street, a dark brown shoulder bag banging against her left hip. She wore her long hair straight back; a gold hair clip secured it in place. Her copper colored face looked serious but was not unattractive; the gray blouse and blue shirt she wore were plain and out of fashion.

"Rent's due, the car needs some major repairs and Phillip is three months behind in child support payments," Honor muttered, continuing the discussion with herself that had started earlier in her office. "I've got five dollars in my pocket and no food in the house. What can I fix for dinner?"

She came to a complete stop in the stairwell of the three story brown stucco apartment building where she and her daughter lived. Her short, squat body tensed with anxiety. The headache that had threatened all day broke out of hiding like bullets fired from a gun.

She mentally inventoried the contents of her kitchen cabinets, refrigerator and freezer. Nothing came to mind until she remembered the package of pinto beans she always kept in case of an emergency in a ceramic jar along with half-filled bags of pasta, brown sugar and shelled nuts.

The beans would cover them for a few days – that was a relief. For some reason she always dreaded having to cook beans. At first she thought it was because she believed that poor people had to eat beans. Eating beans meant you didn't have money to buy something better to cook, but that excuse wasn't right. Beans also reminded her of the women who raised her; Aunt Lila and Iona were excellent cooks, their cooking secrets always came with a pinch of advice.

Honor could remember when she was a young girl she'd sit in front of a stove for hours watching a pot of beans cook. Aunt Lila once told her that "time heals all things."

Now why would she remember what Lila told her about time healing all things when she had so many other memories of them cooking together? She made a left turn down a dim hallway and just two doors down from the apartment she shared with Rosie, she smelled something burning.

Linda's burning something again, Honor thought as she opened the door to Apartment 25.

Linda was a teenage mother who had recently moved in with her boyfriend. She often asked Honor how to cook simple dishes and appeared in Honor's doorway in tears when she burned her first attempt at an expensive pot roast.

The smell did not come from Linda's apartment.

Standing inside her living room, Honor shivered. She felt cold and was reminded of old people who knew that when their joints ached the weather would turn bad.

She dropped everything in her hurry to reach the kitchen; banging her knee on the hand-me-down coffee table and tripping over the floor lamp she'd bought at a rummage sale a few years ago. Halfway to the kitchen she was met by her daughter. Rosie's face was stained with tears.

"What's going on?" She yelled and grabbed Rosie by the arms, shaking her.

Her daughter's thin body shook. She was dressed in blue jeans and a white T-shirt that said "U BET" in large red lottors across the front. On her feet were battered no-brand tennis shoes. Her hair was in braids and small, gold stud earrings decorated her ears.

194

"Mom, I didn't mean to burn the beans, honest," Rose whimpered through her tears as she tried to pull away from Honor's tight clutch.

Honor tightened her hold and stared into her daughter's unhappy face. She could not believe what she had just heard. Dinner was ruined! The headache blossomed and she closed her eyes and repeated, in a daze, "Burnt beans, burnt beans....."

She opened her eyes to a scene from her past; 10-year-old Honor stood by a kitchen table listening to her mother, Ruby.

"Honor, cook these pinto beans for supper tonight," her mother was saying. "I've got to go out now, but I'll be back and I expect supper to be ready when I get home."

Honor watched her mother as she rummaged around in her black handbag, looking for matches or a lighter to light the Camel cigarette that hung from the side of her Revlon red lips. Still talking, Ruby started toward the kitchen door, stopped and glanced back at the silent girl.

"Cornbread's already done .... What's the matter with you? You ain't daydreaming again are you?" Before Honor could move Ruby grabbed her by the arm and gave her a hard shake.

"I've warned you before about listening to me when I talk to you, and I've warned you about burning the beans. If you burn super tonight you better have my belt ready when I get back!" Ruby's eyes were hard and bright as they regarded Honor.

"All we got is beans and I mean to stretch them out till the end of the week, do you hear," she gave Honor one more shake and released her.

"Damn kid, can't do nothing right, I ought to send her ass back to Lila." Ruby muttered as she finally found a silver Zippo lighter and applied the flame to the cigarette still dangling from the corner of her mouth. She picked her coat up from a battered armchair in the living room, exhaled smoke and went out the front door allowing it to bang shut behind her.

Honor waited until she heard her mother's Chevy Impala sputter to life and crunch down the gravel driveway before she allowed herself to cry. She stood in front of the kitchen window, tears rolling down her copper colored cheeks, as the taillights of her mother's car disappeared into the rainy Alabama night.

Ruby would punish her for burning supper. She still stung from the whipping she'd received last Saturday for washing white clothes with dark clothes. Ruby's favorite white blouse, with the crocheted collar and fake pearl buttons, turned a merry shade of pink.

Honor remembered the whipping, which was delivered with a piece of old, thick leather strap from a man's belt, caused welts to rise on her legs. She still had to wear long pants so they wouldn't show.

She wiped her eyes with the back of her hand and turned away from the dish-filled kitchen sink. She found the bag of pinto beans in a vase that was filled with other half empty bags of red beans, lima beans and black-eye peas.

She would have to be careful; even though she already knew what to do she read the instructions over again.

Basic Directions for Pinto Beans: Add six cups of hot water to rinsed and drained beans. Simmer one to one and a half hours or until tender, salt and flavor to taste.

Honor selected a large cast iron pot; half filled it with water and placed it on the stove over a medium flame. She went to the freezer and took out a package of bacon, which she removed from the wrapping and rinsed off at the sink. Then she tore open the bag of beans and dumped them into a blue, plastic bowl which she filled with hot water.

After the bacon and beans were washed, she added both to the cast iron pot and checked to make sure enough water covered the beans before placing the heavy top on the pot. So far everything was OK.

For a brief minute she considered the school books that waited on her lumpy bed. She was a conscientious student who made mostly A's and B's and since she didn't have homework due tomorrow, she planned to spend the evening reading.

Honor loved to read. At the bottom of her closet was a small collection of books she kept in a box. "The Hobbit" by J.R.R. Tolkien was her favorite; she picked it up and turned to chapter seven and read…… "The whole place still stinks of dragon…………"

At the end of chapter 15 Honor did indeed smell something unpleasant. She had lost track of the time.

Surprise followed by fear gripped her. She jumped up from the lumpy, quilt covered bed and raced down the dark hallway into the kitchen. Timidly she lifted the lid and was immediately assaulted by the aroma of burnt beans.

"No, no, no. No!"

Her hand jerked away from her body to turn off the stove. The kitchen clock ticked away the minutes; it was 8:30 pm. In less than 30 minutes her mother would be home. Honor covered her face as fear curled up her spine.

Ruby would kill her and be sent back to the institution; she would be dead.

Honor found herself standing in the bathroom; in the medicine cabinet mirror was a stranger who stared back at her from dark brown, dazed eyes. In her right hand the stranger held a butcher knife; her left hand lay in the white porcelain sink covered with red ribbons that extended down from her wrist, ran between her fingers and flowed down the drain.

"We shows it the way out, yes!" Gollum hissed inside her mind.

Rosie's voice pulled Honor back from the nightmare of her childhood. "Mom, I wanted to surprise you with dinner. I'm sorry I burned the beans!"

Honor's eyes focused on Rosie's tear stained face. She blinked and looked around; for a moment she did not know where she was. Then she focused on the stove and the smoking pot that contained a burned mass of beans.

"Mom," Rosie sounded and look concerned, "Mom? Are you alright?"

Honor looked at her daughter and sighed. With her hands on Rosie's arms, she pulled her into a powerful embrace. Instinctively she looked at her left wrist. Several thin, faint lines, spider webbed her brown skin. The thick dark blue vein pulsed as if remembering that long ago night.

She had forgotten! How could she have forgotten the event that had changed the course of her life?

Only now did she remember that on that ugly night long ago, Aunt Lila came to the hospital and never left her side. During the months that followed, she took custody of Honor and helped her forget and heal. She had done a great job; Honor had buried that memory deep down with the many things about her childhood she avoided thinking about.

Honor released Rosie, kissed her on the forehead and wiped away the tears on her daughter's wet face as well as her own tears of release.

Tonight, she had a lot to think about. After all, thanks to the women who raised her, she had a future! She could not let a slime ball, like her boss Henry Garth, hold her back! Tomorrow she would begin searching for a new job, but right now her daughter needed her.

"When I was a girl and burned the beans, Aunt Lila gave me some good advice," Honor said as she guided Rosie toward the stove to explain about full pots of water, low heat and love.

FAMILY FORTUNE

"Mrs.? Are you Mrs.?"

Lila stared at the white man standing on her porch. He didn't look like an insurance man, police man or any kind of bill collector. True, he was sweaty, but so was she after her part-time work at the fabric and mercantile store in Somerville.

At her age, she could work only two days a week to bring in some extra money, but it was Friday night and Lila felt like she'd worked all week. All she wanted to do was sit down somewhere and rest.

"Lord, I'm so tired I ain't got time for no bill man," she grumbled to herself.

But, he didn't look like a bill man. First thing was he didn't have an accent. He spoke like a Northerner, like her grandkids talk now when they come down for summer visits.

Second, he wasn't dressed like a regular everyday working man. Nope, instead of a Sears & Roebuck summer suit or some cheap white muslin shirt all wilted in the heat of the day, the man fidgeting on the porch had on a beautiful crisp white shirt that looked to her experienced eye like a high grade of cotton that had been laundered by professional cleaners and not some overworked wife or careless maid. And the suit, her fingers twitched just itching to stroke the dove gray fabric that hinted of some exotic blend.

"Mrs.?" he asked again and this time he took off his hat and held it in both hands against his chest. That decided it for Lila. The gesture was respectful and courteous, something the local white folks didn't know the meaning of in connection to colored folks.

"Come on in," Lila said holding the screen door open wide. "It sure is hot out today, ain't it? Bet you could use some cold sweet tea?"

"Well, yes, ma'am, if it's no trouble. Let me introduce myself. My name is Jeffery Lansing. I'm visiting here from Illinois."

"That's nice, Mr. Lansing, so you got some kin down here? Wait, before you answer, let's go sit out under my pecan tree in the back yard, plenty of shade out there and we can get comfortable and visit for a spell. That's right, go on over there and sit down – I'll bring us some tea."

Outside under the pecan tree was the best place to send strangers when you didn't have any idea of their true intentions. That's where Lila kept an ax for chopping wood and a hickory-handled knife used for cleaning fish and other such jobs. With those close at hand she felt safe even if Bull Connor came by for a visit!

Lila peeped around the door after filling his glass with special sweet tea ... Everyone loved the teas; her secret was to add some fruit now and then, today it was some strawberries. He didn't appear to be dangerous, sat there nice as you please with his hands caressing the hat in his lap. She wondered what he wanted.

"Here you go, sir, cool sweet tea for a hot afternoon. Now what can I do for you?"

"Well, I'm looking for a Mrs. Lila Black. In Huntsville and in Teluchi I was told she lived off Highway 33." The stranger stood up to take the tea from Lila; she sat down across from him next to the wood pile.

"What you looking for Lila Black for?" Lila was cautious to not give away anything until she made sure what he wanted.

"It's quite a story." Mr. Lansing leaned back in his chair and took a large drink from the frosty glass. He closed his eyes and licked his lips; taking another large sip he set the glass down and asked, "Did you add strawberries to the tea?"

"Why, yes, yes I did. I specialize in my fruit teas. Well it's no secret, I just take whatever fruit is in season and either cook up a syrup that I add to the tea or cut up fresh fruit right into the tea jug." She liked Mr. Lansing already; anybody who complimented the teas was OK with her.

"You must be Mrs. Black!" Mr. Lansing smiled with relief; his posture relaxed into the chair and he laid aside his hat.

"I'm in the right place and if you'll just hear my story it will explain who I am, what I want and why I came all this way to find you." He clasped his hands together and leaned forward.

"Some time ago, in Detroit, one of our employees went to a picnic; I believe he called it a cookout. At the party he sampled something he called homebrew and he claimed it was the best he'd ever tasted. That might have been the end of it except the company he works for, the company I work for and represent today is Nolan Brothers Brewery. Perhaps you've heard of it?" Mr. Lansing uncrossed his legs, unclasped his hands and looked at Lila with an expectant smile.

"Yes, I know of it," but Lila couldn't think why he was in her back yard. She knew about the company; she'd spent a lifetime being around men who drank, mostly anything they could get but sometimes lately they drank store bought instead of homebrews. Also, her nephew and niece lived in Detroit. She wondered again where Mr. Lansing was going with his story.

"Good, good! I'm just about to the point of my story, Mrs. Black. I want you to know that we've spent a considerable amount of time tracking down your family and obtaining information about your history of making fruit homebrews many years ago."

"The party our employee attended was also attended by your nephew, Mr. Luther Ghee. Mr. Ghee contributed the homebrew to the party. Through our employee we managed to obtain more of the beverage for our personal taste testing. Our brew specialists had heard of home recipes before but had never sampled them. They were extremely excited because we have plans to brew a special beer that will have a citrus taste."

Mr. Lansing stopped talking long enough to take another drink of strawberry tea. Lila didn't know what to say, she still made a few batches of homebrew, mostly for Willie's Jay Bird bar but whenever family came home they often requested she make some for them. Luther probably took some back to Detroit with him after his last visit home.

"Now, Mrs. Black, we would like to purchase your recipe for the fruit homebrews. It will give us the rights to produce and market our own brand under Nolan Brothers Brewery label.

"I assume that you will want to have a family member and a lawyer help you make a decision and we encourage you to do just that. You will be given the opportunity to name your price for the recipe after which we can begin negotiations.

"I've prepared some information to leave with you that includes names and numbers you can contact after you have time to think about the offer. Please know that you will be treated more than fairly by our company. We admire what you have done and we want the world to taste your creation!"

SAYING GOODBYE TO LILA

"Rosie Ghee."

My little girl walked proudly forward and received the honorary handshake with her right hand from the California State University Long Beach president and the Bachelors of Arts degree with her left hand.

I stood up, jumped up and down and yelled, "That's my baby!" My best girlfriend, Miranda, yelled right along with me. Aunt Iona sat more composed but still cheered and clapped just as loudly as we did. We all hugged each other and tried to be quiet for the remainder of the graduation ceremonies.

Miranda and Jackie, a friend from work, joined me and Aunt Iona at the graduation celebration that evening. I had rented out a small section of the Quiet Cannon Restaurant to host Rosie's graduation dinner.

Rosie stood at the front of the table to address all the well wishes and comments that our family and friends made as we raised our glasses and toasted her future. Our path to this day had not been easy but it had been worth everything to see her now.

The little girl with the braids and freckles was now a polished and strong young woman. She wore a white lace dress with her hair piled on top of her head and directed her remarks to me.

"Mom, I appreciate all your dedication these many years. I know that you have sacrificed for me and that everything you did was to make sure that I became a woman that you could be proud of. I raise my glass to you! You deserve this moment as much as me!" She and everyone at the table stood and toasted me.

The tears would not stop falling. Even later as I said goodnight to the many friends who joined us, tears still formed and welled out of my red, puffy eyes. Miss Independent Rosie, with one last kiss, left with her boyfriend, Franklin, to continue their celebrations without the presence of nosy older folks.

I dropped Aunt Iona off at her place and drove home thinking only of changing clothes, taking a shower and heading off to bed. Opening the front door I noticed the light blinking on the answering machine in the living room. I ignored it for now; it could only be other friends or family calling to offer congratulations to Rosie. I followed through with my original plans and changed my clothes followed by a hot shower.

In bed I finally pushed the message button and was not surprised to hear Uncle Junior's voice.

"Hey, Honor, I know this is a great day for you. Me and Billie hope Rosie got our graduation gift. You know we ain't much for traveling these days, neither one of us like flying. But we happy for you and Rosie and that's why I'm so sorry to bring you sad news on this day that must be the best day in your life."

I sat straight up in bed, dreading what he would say next. I clutched the covers to my chest as if it could ward off any evil that now threatened my family. All the misfortune that had already happened flashed through my mind: mom's insanity and death, my grandfather's death, the fire, my attempt at suicide. Would it never end?

On the phone, Uncle Junior's sad voice continued, "Lila passed away this morning. I been trying to call Iona and left a message for her as well. Can you call me back when you get this message? Me and Billie will be up all night."

The tears welled up and spilled over again, but this time they were tears of sorrow, misery and loss.

SECRETS REVEALED

"Lord, it seems like we never get together for anything now but funerals," Iona complained. "I'm getting old and tired of coming home just for funerals. Last time I came home we buried Aunt Mozelle; Uncle Odean, Ms. EJ, Ms. Dora, Uncle Mitchell, Uncle Joe, Ruby and Mr. Hap all gone and now Aunt Lila too."

Iona, Billie, Pearl, Honor and Willa sat out on the front porch of Lila's shack on an early summer afternoon. Everything was painted in pastel colors of green, rose and yellow; a slight breeze blew across the ladies as they chatted, fanned and drank lemonade.

None of the women who sat out on Lila's front porch lived around The Hollow any longer. Lila had been the last of the Ghee line still living on the land and her family had come home to lay her to rest.

Willa's family made their home in Pontiac, Michigan; she had been joined by Luther who now had a family of his own.

Billie and Junior lived in Huntsville and when Joe died, Mozelle moved in with them until her death five years ago.

Early and Pearl settled in Washington D.C. Early was single again after seven years of marriage and two children. Pearl was the one the family was proud of; after completing her education at Alabama A&M, she moved to Atlanta and attended Spelman College where she met her husband

Paul. They both worked in government positions and were doing well. The entire family was proud of them.

Walker, Mason, Iona, Honor and her daughter Rosie lived in California. Honor rarely returned home after Lila sent her to live with Iona so she could attend college. Ruby had already been institutionalized and soon managed to steal enough painkillers and sleeping pills to end her life at the age of 31.

"I'm glad that you all could be here today – all of us together as Ghee women," Iona said.

Looking over them all, Iona could tell by their expressions that none of them were expecting what she had to say, but it was time. Time she got off her chest before too long the secrets she'd kept all these years. Nothing good came of keeping secrets.

Besides, if what she had to share could keep her family together and heal the women, she had to tell them everything before it was too late. Already she felt her body giving out; growing old wasn't for sissies that was sure!

It was time.

She started by confirming suspicions that Lee Ghee had molested, or attempted to molest, at least one female in their family for each of the five generations that she could remember: Maria, Lou Ella, Lila, Willa and Honor.

She started, not at the beginning but somewhere closer to the middle, with a truth that would be a revelation to a few of them.

"Lee Ghee was my uncle and my father."

Looking around at the women, Iona saw mixed emotions. She was thankful that her only child, Mason, was a man and was not included in this discussion. If the women wanted to share with the men they could do so; it would be their choice. With freedom came choices.

Billie, Junior's wife, was the most shocked. She had not grown up in the family, only came to it by marriage. Iona doubted that Junior knew all that had gone on, if he had he had not shared it with Billie. Pearl, Lila's daughter, looked bewildered but not shocked. Iona knew that Lila had not shared much with her either.

Honor and Willa who had been affected and hurt the most returned her look with a grim acceptance. They reached out to each other and held hands.

Billie and Pearl asked questions, but Iona ignored the questions and unfolded a letter that Lila left for her. It explained everything, including a few things Iona had not known about either.

Looking into the eyes of each woman, she could see that they were ready to hear the truth. Iona began to read Lila's letter, hoping that the words would bring them freedom, closure and peace and erase forever any guilt they felt about what happened when they were innocent girls.

As she read she could hear Lila speaking through the words:

"I'm sorry I'm not there with all of you. No long grievin' for me, ladies, please. I'm at peace and believe I'm gonna be with my Lord. I hope that I done some good in my life. I know I did the best I could as a poor country girl who grew up with nothing but secrets, shame and sin.

"I hope Iona is with y'all now. I apologize if this duty fell to someone else. I shared these things with Iona a long time ago, and she shared a few things with me. Baby thank you for helpin' me put this letter together and figurin' out how to finally speak up on the pain and misery us Ghee women went through.

"Since this is just for us, I can speak clearly. Unlike the monies I received from my homebrew recipes and shared with the rest of the family, I only share this with you all.

"There is so much I kept to myself over the years....hard to know where to start but I guess I'll just go back to mama and Miz Lucille, my daddy's white wife.

"Y'all know the story: Daddy took mama as his outside woman until Miz Lucille die and they could get married, 'course they kept that a secret until after he died. You know how we got the land, the store and the family house, which use to be somethin' to see; it was grand and finer than some whites had at the time!

"But what you don't know is that Miz Lucille didn't die a natural death. It was an accident that she fell down those steps, but Lee, daddy and mama were responsible for lettin' her die. Lee told me a long time ago, tryin' to keep me under his control, the truth about that day.

"Miz Lucille, like most Southern white ladies, never did call daddy out about mama and the half white children she was havin', but one day things come to a head between her and daddy on the steps in the big house.

"Lee said that daddy and Miz Lucille were arguin' at the top of the stairs and daddy pushed her away from him and she fell down the steps. Lee said he must have been 'bout five years old at the time. He was at the bottom of the steps, in the great hall, waitin' for mama to come back from the hen house.

"When Miz Lucille fell down, Lee say he went to help her but daddy yelled at him to stay away. Lee say she was still alive when mama come back. He say Miz Lucille turned her head towards mama, lifted her hand for help but mama didn't help her either. It took some time before she stopped movin' and lay silent. They just stood there until she die.

"Blood on Lee's hands from the beginnin' I suppose.

"A few of you remember Lou Ella; she was Lee's first wife. In the beginnin' she was so cute, had a heart shaped face. She was in love with Lee so much! But then he raped her little sister Marie, Iona's mother. It damaged Lou so bad she stopped talkin' for a long time.

"Every now and again she would talk and she told me, after my second marriage, that Iona was Lee's child. She told me what happened the night Iona was born; how Marie, with her last breath told her what Lee done to her; he told her he was gonna make her a woman.

"It explained a lot 'bout how she felt about me; I didn't know it at the time but she knew when Truly was born that somethin' was wrong.

"Lou raised Iona like she was her own child -- I Own Her -- and she always watched out for her; keepin' her safe from Lee for the rest of her sad life.

"Now, his second wife was Essie. Whew, she was a spitfire woman and gave him back a bit of what he gave out. Essie was Walker and Ruby's mama.

"That, too, ended in tragedy. Most people think a fight broke out 'tween Essie and Lou and they kill each other. By the time I got to the family house that night, they both dead and Lee had blood on his shirt and pants.

"Now the truth of what happened is Lou found out about what Lee done to Willa and for her that was the last straw. Willa already told Iona what he done and the two of them figured out a way to keep her away from him for a while, but eventually he caught her alone and forced her again. That's when Willa decided to run away and Iona was gone help her.

"The night they decided to take off Lou caught Iona sneakin' out the house and would not let her go; Iona say she give in and told her everythang. He'd been on Willa about two years; poor thang couldn't take it anymore. Well, Lou left the house and told Iona she would handle it and they wouldn't have to worry none about him anymore.

"The fight may have started out 'tween the three of them. Essie may have been tryin' to defend Lee, that's why I think she was the first to go down; she may have died first. I think

Lee killed Lou to be done with her and put an end to what she knew about what he done to Marie, me and Willa. He the one say they killed each other, he was the only witness. I never saw him grieve for neither one of them.

"Oh, my, I'm glad not to take these things with me to my grave. Thank you again, Iona, for hearin' the truth about our family, for helpin' me let go of the pain.

"Now it's my turn to let the others know what Lee done to me, his own sister.

"When our bother Thom was hanged by the Klan and Lou Ella's brother died in a fire set by the Klan, mama wanted me away from everythang so I would be safe. I was sent to live with relatives until after I was a teenager. I come home just before mama die.

"I wish I could say when Lee first started to put his hands on me, but lookin' back it musta started fairly early. He would touch me and linger on certain parts of my body as he talked about what he called my trainin' in becoming a woman.

"It wasn't until I come back home that he followed up on my final training. It was before my first marriage. None of y'all, 'cept Iona and Willa, remember my first husband Ben Taylor or Baby Truly.

"Lee took me before I married Ben, and I went into that marriage thinkin' that the awful things he done to me were what my husband wanted in a wife. Poor Ben was sweet and gentle, he wanted none of what I thought pleased a

215

man. It was a sad affair and I only realized I loved him after he was dead.

"Baby Truly mighta been Lee's baby. She certainly looked like us Ghee's more than the Taylors. But she was my baby and I loved her, love her still.

"When we finally found out that Lee forced himself on Willa, Mozelle and I made sure she could leave as soon as possible. Mozelle had a friend up north and we got our savings together and put her on a train with a one way ticket. After Willa was gone, Iona decided to move to Madison County. Junior help her get a job and get on her feet.

"Willa, if you are with everyone now, baby, perhaps you want to let it go; these women care for you. If you decide to share, the best way to do it is in their company.

"Iona told me that Lee tried to get her a few times but that he never got a chance to touch her. I'm so thankful for that. I'm not sure about Ruby. She never said so and I never had reason to believe he did. She had enough to live with, God rest her soul.

"That ends what I have to tell. Many of you know Honor's story. It is one that she can choose to talk about now as well.

"May God help me but I could never forgive Lee for what he done to us. I'm sorry, but I feel the fire was the justice he deserved.

"When I received the monies from Nolan Brothers Brewery I give Iona, Willa and Honor larger shares of the settlement. It was my way of giving something back to you

216

for the years of pain caused by my brother and that I was not woman enough to speak out. Poor Lou was the only one who tried to do something about it.

"I pray you all forgive me for never standin' up and takin' action against him. I regret that above all things, and I apologize to each of you that I let you down.

"Be at Peace – I finally am. Lila."

      *   *   *   *

After burying Aunt Lila I was eager to get away from The Hollow for good and never come back.

Walking back to my car, I knew this would be the last time I saw this place. Even if time and progress didn't guarantee it, I was now free to let it go.

The old mountain trail was no longer visible. None of the ancestral houses could be seen except for Aunt Lila's tin roof shack. The house, along with the last 25 acres, now belonged to Tennessee Valley Authority and was designated for a wildlife preserve and, as of yesterday, was no longer part of the Ghee future.

Final arrangements had been made to divide the money from the sale of the property between the heads of household.

Aunt Lila's letter revealed all the family secrets we'd kept hidden for five generations. It confirmed all our worst fears but led to freedom and released the Ghee women from any guilt or remorse about the past.

Lila, Iona, Willa and I had been touched the most by the evil of incest and abuse. We finally got to console each other and share the pain, misery and fear that we'd carried around all our lives.

In Aunt Lila's cabin, surrounded by the love we felt for each other and the great relief of her letter, we felt safe enough to talk publicly about what we'd live through privately.

Iona shared how guilty she'd felt that her father, who she thought was her uncle, had been the monster under the bed, how she'd ran rather than confront him and stayed away instead of relieving Lila of the burdens she kept from the family.

Willa shared the details of the times Lee violated her; how she'd first enjoyed the attentions of someone she viewed as a father figure, but later that enjoyment turned into disgust and self-hatred. Her life had been a series of bad choices, of choosing the wrong men, and acceptance of mistreatment as if she wasn't worthy.

And me, well nothing could take away the image of Lee's burning body or the darkness after my suicide attempt. But I was no longer that girl whose mother had abandoned her, or the child raised by aunts and other family members, wondering what had I done to deserve all the bad things that happened to me; I was no longer hiding in a back room talking to a doll with blue hair.

For many years I'd lived a successful life; with Rosie's graduation and bright future I knew that I'd given her the life I'd never had. Only the past held me bound and now it had been exposed to the light and I was free.

With the sun shining on my face, I breathed in the fresh country air and for the last time turned my back on the land and on the past that was The Hollow.

AFTERWORD

If you or someone you know has experienced sexual abuse, you are not alone. There are 42 million survivors of child sexual abuse in the United States and 20% were abused before age eight according to Darkness to Light, an organization that empowers people to prevent child sexual abuse: www.d2l.org.

Speak Out! The most powerful weapon you can use is to speak up and speak out about what's going on or what has gone on. Speaking up releases the abused one from a prison of secrets and shame and puts the spotlight on the victimizer who may be a family member (90% of victims know their abuser according to Darkness to Light).

The Rape, Abuse & Incest National Network, an anti-sexual assault organizational working with local rape crisis centers across the U.S., states 68% of sexual assaults are not reported to police. www.rainn.org.

The National Sexual Assault Hotline: 800-656-HOPE

www.ingramcontent.com/pod-product-compliance
Lightning Source LLC
Chambersburg PA
CBHW070112260626
47160CB00004B/1435